Caught in the Act

The kitchen door was locked. Undeterred, Fargo hopped to the ground and over to the window. For a moment the window resisted, but then gave way and slid partway open. On the other side of the kitchen, stairs led up to the rented rooms. If he was quiet, he could sneak upstairs and find the girl before anyone was the wiser. He began to wedge himself inside.

Out of nowhere, an iron vise clamped on to Fargo's shoulder. He was ripped loose and thrown to the earth so brutally he thought his ribs were cracked. The world spun. When his vision cleared, he was lying at the foot of a huge, bearded man whose head seemed to brush the clouds.

"You shouldn't have come back, mister," said the giant, reaching down with a pair of bulging, muscular arms. "And now I'm gonna bust you into a million pieces."

THE
TRAILSMAN
#217

DAKOTA
DECEPTION

by

Jon Sharpe

A SIGNET BOOK

SIGNET
Published by New American Library, a division of
Penguin Putnam Inc., 375 Hudson Street,
New York, New York 10014, U.S.A.
Penguin Books Ltd, 27 Wrights Lane,
London W8 5TZ, England
Penguin Books Australia Ltd,
Ringwood, Victoria, Australia
Penguin Books Canada Ltd, 10 Alcorn Avenue,
Toronto, Ontario, Canada M4V 3B2
Penguin Books (N.Z.) Ltd, 182–190 Wairau Road,
Auckland 10, New Zealand

Penguin Books Ltd, Registered Offices:
Harmondsworth, Middlesex, England

First published by Signet, an imprint of New American Library,
a division of Penguin Putnam Inc.

First Printing, November 1999
10 9 8 7 6 5 4 3 2 1

The first chapter of this book originally appeared in *High Sierra Horror,*
the two hundred sixteenth volume in this series.

 REGISTERED TRADEMARK—MARCA REGISTRADA

Printed in the United States of America

The Trailsman

Beginnings . . . they bend the tree and they mark the man. Skye Fargo was born when he was eighteen. Terror was his midwife, vengeance his first cry. Killing spawned Skye Fargo, ruthless, cold-blooded murder. Out of the acrid smoke of gunpowder still hanging in the air, he rose, cried out a promise never forgotten.

The Trailsman they began to call him all across the West: searcher, scout, hunter, the man who could see where others only looked, his skills for hire but not his soul, the man who lived each day to the fullest, yet trailed each tomorrow. Skye Fargo, the Trailsman, and the seeker who could take the wildness of a land and the wanting of a woman and make them his own.

1861—the Dakota Territory, where lies
and bullets fly thick and fast and where family ties
are sometimes bound too tightly. . . .

"Quit squirming. I can't concentrate on my cards."

The luscious dove perched on Skye Fargo's lap wasn't the only reason he was having trouble concentrating. Whiskey was also to blame, enough to stagger a bull elk. Fargo squinted at his poker hand, willing his numb mind to focus. He had three jacks and two fours. A full house. "I'll see you, and raise you another fifty," he announced, shoving a pile of chips to the center of the table.

Sally Crane giggled. "Win this pot, handsome, and you'll have cleaned everyone else out. Isn't that wonderful?"

Across from Fargo sat a player who didn't think so. His name was Gar Myers. He was a big bear of a riverman, one of those rowdy ruffians who made their living on the steamboats that plied the broad Missouri River. His cheeks were red from anger as well as from alcohol, and he glared murderously at Fargo from under bushy brows. "I've never seen such a streak of luck in all my born days. Some might say you're a little *too* lucky."

Fargo tensed. The insult was plain enough, and it was one no frontiersman would stand for. But before he could reply, Sally spoke, wagging a painted fingernail.

"That's enough out of you, Gar. Skye hasn't been cheating, and you damn well know it. Hell, he's had his best hands when it wasn't his turn to deal. So leave him be."

The other two players had already folded and were awaiting the outcome. One, an elderly character in overalls and a floppy hat, snickered. "If you're lookin' to blame someone, Gar, blame yourself. You're about the worst poker player alive. You can't bluff for beans, and every time you get a good hand you give it away by grinnin' like an idiot."

"Shut up, you old buzzard," Gar grated. Consulting his cards, he gnawed on his thick lower lip a moment, then added the last of his chips to the pile. "All right. There you go, mister. Now let's see what you've got."

Fargo swiveled, motioning for Sally to slide off of his lap. Pouting as she rose, she made sure to brush her bosom lightly across his cheek, trying to entice him, just as she had been doing all evening. It wasn't hard to guess what she had in mind for later.

"I don't have all night," Gar said, raising his voice much louder than was called for. His dark eyes gleamed with sinister resentment.

"Hold your horses," Fargo said. Shifting again, so the Colt on his right hip was within easy reach, he proceeded to lay out his cards, one by one, watching the riverman closely. Gar's bulging cheeks grew darker and a storm cloud roiled on his brow. The man fidgeted like a steam engine set to explode.

"*Another* full house? Damn! How many does that make? Three this whole game? That isn't natural!"

Fargo placed his hands on the edge of the table. The other men were poised for flight should trouble start. At nearby tables, players had stopped what they were doing to watch. "Say it plainly."

Gar smacked his cards down. He had three queens. "Fine by me. I think you cheat!" And with that, the riverman heaved upward, upending the table in one quick movement.

Fargo tried to skip aside but his sluggish reflexes hampered him. The table crashed into his chest, knocking him backward. Stumbling, he fell, the table landing on top of him while cards and chips spilled everywhere. He heard men yell, lusty curses, then the table was pulled away and Gar loomed above him, his brawny hands reaching for his shirt. Fargo started to go for the Colt, then realized the riverman was unarmed. Shooting the bastard would bring the law down on his head, and that was the last thing Fargo wanted.

"I'm going to bust your skull!" Gar raged.

As iron fingers lifted him off the floor, Fargo galvanized to life. His right fist swept up, catching Myers flush on the jaw. It was like hitting an anvil. Gar only smiled, then threw Fargo into another table.

Players scattered. More shouts broke out. The table stayed upright but Fargo didn't, his boots off the floor as he sprawled across the playing table. Gar was on him again in a twinkling. A fist rammed into Fargo's stomach, another into his ribs. Anger cleared Fargo's head, and he retaliated with a right cross that jolted the big riverman, giving Fargo the precious seconds he needed to stand.

The bartender was bellowing for them to stop. Gar paid no heed. Balling his ham-sized fists, he advanced, lumbering like a grizzly, confident in his size and his power. "I'll enjoy stomping you to mush," he boasted.

Fargo delivered an uppercut, sidestepped, and followed through with a jab to the man's midsection. The riverman lashed out with a backhand which he nimbly avoided. Then, as Gar pivoted, Fargo landed a solid left to Gar's temple that sent the big man tottering.

"That's showin' him!" the old-timer whooped. "Do it again!"

Fargo began to glide in close but stopped when Gar straightened, blood lust animating his brutish features.

"You hit hard, mister. Harder than anyone I can recollect. But it'll take more than one lucky punch to drop me. I've gone toe to toe with six men at once, and won."

Fargo didn't doubt it. The riverman was big enough, and strong as an ox. But size and strength weren't always enough to win a fight, as Fargo now demonstrated by gliding forward, ducking under a jab, and slamming a blow to the gut that folded Gar like an accordion.

3

Gar grunted, the breath whooshing from his lungs like spray from a geyser. Fargo gave him no time to recover. He struck once, twice, three times, and Gar went down, falling back onto a chair, which shattered like so much kindling.

Excitement had gripped the saloon's patrons, and many were encouraging their favorite. Some wanted Fargo to win, others bawled for Gar to get back up. One of the loudest was Sally, who shrieked at Fargo, "Bash his stupid noggin in!"

That wouldn't be easy. Myers had a skull as thick as a buffalo's. Shaking his head to clear it, the riverman surged upright and came at Fargo like a grizzly gone amok. Shoulders lowered, he snorted as he charged.

Fargo tried to leap aside but he was hemmed in by tables and chairs. Gar drove into his abdomen like a battering ram, lifting him clear off his feet. Yet another table bore the brunt of their fall. Fargo attempted to scramble erect but Gar's enormous hands pinned him down. A knee missed his groin by an inch, numbing his left leg and sending searing pain throughout his body.

"Now I've got you!" the riverman declared.

Knuckles the size of walnuts flashed toward Fargo's face. At the last instant he jerked his head to the right and Gar's fist smashed into the floorboards. Gar howled and drew his arm back, enabling Fargo to lock his hands together and swing them as he would a club. He pounded Gar on the neck, on the ear, and on the nose. The last blow had the desired effect. Gar pushed off of him, dazed but far from finished, as Fargo rose.

The onlookers had formed a circle, a ring of sweaty faces eager to see blood spilled. Out of the corner of an eye Fargo noticed three people who were standing off by themselves, near the entrance. Dressed in the height of fashion, they didn't share the crowd's general enthusiasm. Two were men whose expressions were as cold as ice. The third, a beautiful redhead, had her cherry mouth curled in a contemptuous sneer. She was worth closer scrutiny, but just then Gar roared and hurled forward.

"Damn you, little man!"

No one had ever called Fargo "little" before. He was big in his own right. Maybe not as bulky or as broad as the riverman, but he packed solid sinew on his pantherish frame. A lifetime of living in the wilderness had sculpted his body much like a whetstone honed a knife. He proved as much now by agilely evading Gar's headlong rush and hammering Gar twice as the lummox barreled by.

When Gar spun back around, his mouth was dripping scarlet drops and he was wheezing like a bellows. "No one bloodies me," he growled. His hand dipped into his shirt and came out with a glittering dagger.

The saloon promptly fell quiet.

"None of that!" the old-timer called out. "Keep it fair! It ain't a fight to the death!"

"Isn't it?" Gar said, and attacked.

The dagger flicked like a striking rattler. Fargo managed to spring backward out of harm's reach but Gar wasn't to be denied. Swinging wildly, the riverman bore down like a runaway wagon. Fargo danced to one side, then the other, always one stride ahead of cold steel. He bumped into a chair, gripped it, and slid it across the floor at Myers. A swat of the man's huge hand sent it skidding away.

"It'll take more than that to stop me!" Gar boomed. His wide, bloodshot eyes seemed to glow as he came in for the kill.

Fargo let him. He waited until the riverman was almost on top of him, then he drew the Colt. No one would blame him if he gunned Gar down. Everyone had seen Gar pull out the dagger. But he didn't shoot, not with so many by-standers, any one of whom might catch a stray slug. He rapped the barrel across Gar's hand, eliciting a yip of raw agony, forcing Gar to drop the weapon. Then he unleashed a battering flurry, smashing the barrel against Gar's temples, pistol-whipping him savagely.

Gar began to buckle. He brought his arms up to protect himself but Fargo battered them, too. Staggered, Gar attempted to turn and run.

Fargo wouldn't relent. He kept on pistol-whipping the riverman until Gar was on his knees, swaying like a reed in the wind, blood pouring from a dozen gashes. A score of nasty welts were added evidence of the severe beating he was taking. Fargo elevated his arm high overhead, then swept it down one last time. There was the sickening sound of metal connecting with flesh and bone, followed by a thud as the unconscious riverman sprawled in a miserable heap.

Breathing heavily, Fargo slowly lowered the revolver, then twirled it into his holster. No one else spoke as he went to the overturned table and squatted to gather up his winnings. A pair of shapely legs wreathed in a tight patterned dress materialized before him and a warm hand stroked his neck.

"You were terrific, handsome. But if it had been me, I'd have plugged him. Gar isn't likely to forget and he sure as hell won't forgive."

Fargo absently nodded. Right now all he wanted was to buy another bottle of rotgut and take Sally Crane to the hotel for a night of frolicking under the sheets. It had been weeks since he visited civilization and treated himself to the exquisite pleasure of a willing woman. And Sally certainly was willing. The moment she'd laid eyes on him, she'd sashayed over with a warm smile. That was hours ago.

"Here. I'll lend you a hand."

The brunette hunkered, the sweet fragrance of her perfume enough to set Fargo's mouth to watering. The swell of her ample breasts, her flat stomach, the equally enticing curve of her hips and the hint of treasures lower down were enough to set his manhood to stirring. A lump formed in his throat.

Sally was busy retrieving chips while doing what she did

best: babbling. "Beats me why men like Gar bother to gamble. Poor losers shouldn't be allowed to play cards. Why, just last week a settler tried to cut a local gambler, and had his own throat slit for his effort. Men can be so silly."

So could women, Fargo reflected, but he kept his pearl of wisdom to himself. The old-timer and the other player joined them, helping out.

"That sure was a sight for sore eyes, Trailsman," the geezer commented merrily. "If I were twenty years younger, I'd have done it myself long ago."

Sally looked up. "Trailsman? Why did you call him that?"

The old man tittered. "Hellfire, girl. Don't you know anything? This gent is plumb famous. He's just about the best scout and trail finder who ever lived." He grinned at Fargo. "I saw you once about two years ago, over at Fort Randall. A lieutenant pointed you out. That was right after you'd set up a parley with Moon Killer. Remember?"

Fargo recollected it well. Moon Killer was a renegade, a half-breed who had organized a band of cutthroats and then had gone on a spree of pillage and plunder. Two years ago Moon Killer had taken a white girl captive. The army had asked for Fargo's help in getting her back, so Fargo had gotten word to the killer through a trader, letting Moon Killer know that the girl's father was willing to pay ten thousand dollars for her safe return. Moon Killer had sent the girl's ears and nose, wrapped in her scalp.

Sally was studying Fargo with renewed interest. "Well, I'll be. I've never bedded anyone famous before. Unless you count that senator from back East who was taking a steamboat trip last summer. Now there was a talker! He used so many big words, my head was spinning. Had me believing he was the greatest lover since the dawn of time. But we hadn't hardly taken our clothes off when he fell asleep."

"That's a politician for you," the old-timer quipped. "If hot air was gold, they'd all be rich."

The saloon was returning to normal. All the tables and chairs had been rearranged, Gar Myers had been dragged out, and conversations were resuming. The bartender was wiping blood from the floor with the same grimy cloth he had used to wipe the glasses clean.

"Say, Trailsman," the old man said, "it ain't none of my business, I know. But I was wonderin'. Are you here after Moon Killer? I hear tell he struck again last week, just a short ways north of Yankton."

"He did?" Sally said.

"Yes, ma'am. The army is keepin' it hush-hush. They sent out a patrol, hopin' they could catch him off guard. But that vermin has more lives than a cat. He'll get clean away, like he always does."

Fargo gathered up the last of his chips. "I'm not here after Moon Killer," he revealed as he stood up. Truth was, he was only passing through. He'd had no intention of staying in Yankton more than a day. But when he'd heard about the grand celebration, he'd decided it was worth his while to stick around.

It wasn't every day the U.S. Congress established a new territory. For years the settlers in that region had been begging Congress to act, and now finally, their wish had been granted. The Dakota Territory, as it was called, stretched from the Missouri River to Canada and from the mighty Mississippi to the Rockies. Yankton, which boasted a paltry few hundred inhabitants, had been made the capital.

Small wonder the citizenry was in a festive mood. For almost a week they had indulged in a spree of nonstop drinking, long-winded speeches, horse races, shooting matches, dances, and more.

Fargo had made the most of the situation. He'd won a sizeable poke at cards and faro, made the acquaintance of several ravishing fallen angels, and was on a first-name basis with most of the bartenders. The Lucky Dollar had been the only saloon left to visit, and when he'd strolled in earlier he'd been looking for a good time, not a fight.

Arching his spine to relieve a kink, Fargo walked to the bar. "A new bottle," he instructed the bartender, a balding chunk of beef who sported a waxed mustache half a foot long.

"Care for a little advice to go with it?" the barkeep asked as he stepped to a shelf crammed with an assortment of bottles. Without waiting for Fargo to answer, he went on. "Better watch your back from here on out. Gar Myers won't rest until he's carved his initials in your forehead. Savvy?"

"Let him try," Fargo said. He'd tangled with more than his share of hard cases like Myers. It wasn't worth losing sleep over.

"The thing is," the bartender said, "he won't come alone. He's part of a rough pack, five or six of the most vicious river rats anywhere. If I know him, he'll round up as many of them as he can find and hunt you down."

"I'll be on the lookout," Fargo promised. Accepting the red-eye, he turned and was surprised to find the trio he had noticed before now barring his way. "You're in my road," he informed them.

The taller of the two men cleared his throat. He wore a high hat that crowned neatly combed brown hair cropped just above a frilled white shirt. His jacket and trousers were the best money could buy, as was the short cloak draped over his shoulders and the long cane he carried in his gloved right hand. "Pardon our intrusion, but *are* you Skye Fargo? The tracker and scout?"

It was Fargo's night for being recognized. Beyond them, Sally beckoned and started to amble toward the batwing doors, her hips jiggling seductively. Adopting his best poker face, Fargo said, "You must have me confused with someone else." He stepped to move past the threesome but they stayed put.

"That can't be," the tall dandy said. "The proprietor of a saloon across the street pointed you out to us this morning."

"He was wrong." Fargo saw Sally give him the sort of inviting look that most men would gladly die for.

9

The redhead who was with the two highbreds pursed those cherry lips of hers. "Evidently he was. You're nothing more than a drunkard and brawler."

"That's me." Fargo held his own. "And loving every minute of it." He shouldered past them. "Now if you'll excuse me, I have more living to do." But he only took a single step when a hand fell on his shoulder and he was spun around by the last member of the threesome, a short, stocky man with a nose almost as broad as it was long and a chin that jutted like a stalagmite.

"Hold on, lout. I don't like your tone. Apologize for your rude behavior or I'll thrash you within an inch of your life." He, too, held a cane, which he brandished threateningly.

Fargo sighed. It was also his night for running into jackasses. "Tell you what," he said, anxious to be off. "Look me up tomorrow and I'll gladly knock your teeth down your throat. But right now, I'm busy." Winking at the redhead, he rotated and was gone before they could object.

Sally was waiting at the doors. "What was that all about? I didn't know you knew the Weldons."

"The who?"

"Charlotte Weldon and her two cousins, Gordon and Finlay. They showed up about two weeks ago searching for someone or other. Wealthy as can be, the word is. And as hifalutin as the day is long."

Fargo looped his free arm around her waist and pulled her close. "Forget about them. Let's go." His stomach rumbled, reminding him he hadn't eaten since breakfast. But his craving for food paled in comparison to his craving for Sally Crane's charms. Arm in arm they walked along the dirt-encrusted boardwalk, wending through the throngs of people out taking the evening air. At the end of the dusty street, on a grassy knoll, a band was playing near long tables heaped high with food. It was the last night of the celebration. After the meal there would be another dance, and fireworks were to be shot off.

Sally said longingly, "I'd sure like to attend the get-together tonight. Music, the stars, and you in my arms. That would be heaven on earth."

"I bet you tell that to all your admirers," Fargo said, and received a playful smack to the shoulder.

"For your information, I'm very particular about who I spend my free time with. I get paid to let men paw me, but there are limits to how much pawing I'll allow." Sally softened and pecked him on the nose. "In your case, there's no limit. I probably shouldn't admit it, but I took a fancy to you the second you walked into the Lucky Dollar."

"Must be my buckskins," Fargo joked. They were ragged, in need of repair. Or better yet, he should treat himself to a whole new pair.

Sally chuckled. "Sorry, but I prefer suits and shirts." She ran her fingers through his hair, careful not to bump off his hat. "No, it's your damn good looks that won me over. I swear, but a gal could lose herself in those lake blue eyes of yours."

Her eyes were nothing to sneeze at, either, Fargo mused. A hazel shade, they were twin pools of smoldering desire. For him. He inhaled her musky perfume and lightly kissed her on the throat.

"So how about it?" she inquired.

"How about what?"

"Taking me to the dance, you scatter-brain? Please. I've never asked this of any fella. It would really mean a lot to me."

Fargo balked. He had no hankering to while away hours at a town social. But the plea in her eyes touched him more deeply than he would admit. She was sweet, considerate, and playful. Just the sort of woman he liked. Bringing her a little happiness was worth it in light of what she was going to share with him later on.

"It's not as if I'm asking you to tie yourself to my apron strings. All I want is to dance a bit, laugh a bit. Like I used to do when I was a girl. Before my folks died and I had to make my own way in this world."

"I'll do it," Fargo said.

Sally halted so abruptly she nearly tripped. Her face lit up like the bonfire that was built for the occasion. "Honestly and truly? You're not just saying that?"

Fargo was about to assure her he was in earnest when once again a hand clamped onto his shoulder, and once again he was spun around to confront the three Weldons from back East.

The short one with the jutting chin had done the honors. "You lied to us, sir," he snapped.

"Did I?"

"Most definitely. The bartender at the Lucky Dollar confirmed that you are, indeed, Skye Fargo, the individual we seek. I demand an explanation. And an apology."

"Do you?" Fargo's temper was frayed from his clash with the riverman. He'd been imposed on enough for one night. Casually handing the whiskey bottle to Sally, he suddenly punched the dandy rooster, who teetered back into the taller man. Both struck a hitch rail. Instantly, the taller one recovered and coiled to spring.

"No, Finlay! Enough!" Charlotte Weldon, the ravishing redhead, stepped between them. "How can we ever expect him to work for us if we assault him like common ruffians?"

The short man, Gordon, had regained his footing, his broad nostrils flaring like those of a riled longhorn. "We'll find someone else. No one lays a finger on me. Ever. The code requires that I issue a challenge, and by God, that's exactly what I intend to do."

This time it was Finlay Weldon who intervened. "Desist, brother. Charlotte is right. We've overstepped ourselves."

"I don't care," Gordon fumed. "He caught me off guard but that won't happen again. I'll split him like a melon." Gripping the silver handle of his cane, he started to twist it.

Charlotte Weldon rounded on him with venom in her voice and spite in her eyes. "Not another word, cousin, or you'll answer to me! In case you've forgotten, I am in charge. Either do as I say or pack your bags and catch the next steamboat to St. Louis."

Gordon reluctantly lowered his cane but his nose continued to flare.

"Now then," Charlotte said, pivoting and mustering a smile, "why don't we start over?" She offered her hand.

"Why don't the three of you go to hell?" Deliberately, Fargo took Sally's hand instead and led the dove toward the knoll. They would eat, and dance, and go to the hotel, and by morning he would be well rested and raring to leave Yankton. It would be nice to be out on the open prairie again. He'd had enough of so-called civilization to last him a good long spell.

"Oh dear," Sally said, coming to a stop. "Maybe this wasn't such a good idea, after all." She pointed straight ahead.

Fargo looked. Storming toward them, charging through the crowd like the prow of a ship through the sea, was the big riverman, Gar Myers, and a couple of flinty-eyed companions.

2

Skye Fargo instinctively lowered his hand to his Colt. Then he noticed that Gar hadn't spotted him yet, and that the riverman was gazing at something or someone on the other side of the street. A narrow gap between two buildings yawned to the left. Fargo immediately pulled Sally Crane into it. They had to stand chest to bosom, her ripe mouth mere inches from his.

"What in the world?" she blurted. "Can't you wait, you randy goat?"

"Gar," Fargo explained. The feel of her breasts and thighs aroused him mightily. Combined with the effects of the whiskey, his manhood surged to attention.

Sally glanced down and smirked. "Oh, really? Or is that just your excuse?"

Boots clomping heavily by caused Fargo to cover her mouth with his hand. Within seconds Gar and his men had gone by. Fargo waited until their footsteps had faded, then he carefully peeked out. "They're making for the Lucky Dollar." Once they learned he was gone they'd scour Yankton from end to end. But with everyone out and about, odds were they wouldn't find him.

They hurried on. Already scores of people had gathered to hear the band and partake of the delicious fare spread on the tables, with more arriving every minute. Many of the men gave Sally second looks. Fargo couldn't blame them.

Sally Crane was the kind of woman who provoked a deep yearning in any hot-blooded male. Her face, a perfect oval, was as beautiful as could be. Her hair, done up in curls and brushed back at the front, was lustrous in the lantern light. And her form-fitting dress, cut low to accent the swell of her ample mounds, only added to her allure. The floral pattern seemed to writhe with every movement she made, as if the flowers were alive. Black velvet trim adorned the hem and sleeves of the garment. All told, she possessed a sensual air that was extremely stimulating.

Sally tugged on his arm and nodded at where several couples were dancing to a slow melody being played by the four musicians. "Let's dance first."

"On an empty stomach?"

Fargo escorted her to the tables. A line had formed, and each person was helping himself to whatever he liked. Fargo marveled at the selection. The meat dishes alone were enough to make his stomach rumble anew. There was ham, garnished with greens and dripping with its own juices. There was venison, superbly prepared, and piles of elk meat. There was a platter of roast beef, a rarity in those parts. Even a plate heaped high with fish.

"I'm really not that hungry," Sally remarked.

Fargo was famished—so much so, it was hard to choose what to take and what not to. Fresh bread, layered thick with butter. Buns covered with sticky icing. Vegetables stacked in heaps, carrots and beans and beets, cabbage and lettuce, potatoes cooked whole and mashed. He treated himself to corn on the cob, a slab of beef an inch thick, and three slices of bread.

Sally settled for a spoonful of green beans, a thin strip of ham, and a roll.

Under a spreading oak tree, Fargo held her plate while she sat, then he plopped down with his back against the trunk. She had been holding on to the whiskey bottle, and now she set it to one side.

Fargo lifted his fork to begin. Without warning a shadow fell across them. Thinking the worst, he snatched for his pistol. Only it wasn't Gar Myers. A thin, middle-aged man in a black frock coat and a stiff white collar was appraising them through spectacles that reflected the flickering flames of a nearby lantern.

"Parson!" Sally exclaimed. "I haven't seen you in a while."

"Through no fault of mine, my dear," the minister said, smiling. "The church is still where it's always been."

Sally Crane blushed. "Oh. Well, you see, I've been so busy of late, I just haven't had the time—" To change the subject, she placed a hand on Fargo and introduced him. "This is Pastor Adams. He's been trying to save me in spite of myself."

"Parson," Fargo greeted him, hoping they weren't in for a lecture on wayward women and those who associated with them.

"I trust you two will have a fine time this evening," the minister said. "But I would take it as a personal favor if you would do so without that." He pointed at the bottle.

"I paid good money for it," Fargo mentioned.

"No doubt. But in the flyers we posted, we specifically asked folks not to bring any hard liquor." Pastor Adams held out his hand. "Please, sir. I enjoy a little nip now and then myself. But whiskey has no place here. Too much alcohol leads to arguments and fights, and we want this to be a peaceful social."

Sally nudged Fargo. "Go on. Give it to him. We can get by without it."

"I'll hold it for you at the church," the minister said. "You're welcome to stop and pick it up anytime." Swiveling, he indicated a stern-visaged woman whose arms were filled with bottles and flasks. "We already have quite a collection. Scotch, ale, you name it. I could open my own saloon."

Pastor Adams and Sally chortled. Frowning, Fargo handed the whiskey over.

"I'm grateful, sir. To be frank, I'd rather someone else have this chore. But the council thought that I was the only one who could enforce their edict and not be shot. Some fellows become downright testy when you try to take their liquor away."

"Can't imagine why," Fargo said dryly.

"May you both know true happiness in time and eternity," Pastor Adams said, departing. "And, Miss Crane, I'll expect you at services this weekend. It has been far too long."

"I'll be there." Sally bit into the roll. "Isn't he just the sweetest man? He'd never harm a soul. It's too bad more people aren't like him."

Fargo's annoyance faded. The minister had a point. A lot of families were present, many with small children. It was no place for rowdy behavior. Permitting alcohol would be like lighting a fuse and waiting for the powder keg to explode. Besides, he'd already had more than enough. He should be thankful his head had cleared sufficiently for him to think straight.

The mouth-watering aroma of the beef brought Fargo's reverie to an end. He ate with relish, savoring every bite. It wasn't often he had homemade cooking. It gave him a whole new appreciation for married men, and explained why so many ended up with bellies the size of barrels after ten or twenty years of wedded bliss.

For dessert Fargo selected a huge slice of apple pie. He washed the meal down with three cups of steaming coffee, sweetened with that luxury of luxuries, sugar. Filled to bursting, he stretched and said, "I think I'll take a nap. Wake me in half an hour."

"You'll do no such thing," Sally scolded. "You promised me that we would dance and I'm holding you to it."

"Now?" All the food had made Fargo as sluggish as a snail.

"Right this instant."

Sally hauled Fargo erect and guided him toward a flat area where couples were promenading in a large circle. He began to regret his promise. Dancing wasn't his favorite pastime. Not that he was clumsy at it. He just hadn't danced very often and wasn't familiar with the latest steps. Fortunately, the musicians played a waltz next, so all he had to do was hold Sally close and pretend they were swirling on air.

"My goodness. You sure are light on your feet," she complimented him.

"I don't want to step on yours and be kicked in the shins."

"I'd never," Sally said, laughing. Her cares had melted away, lending her face a radiant sheen. She tilted her head and half closed her eyes, adrift in the melancholy of the violin. "I can't thank you enough, Skye," she said softly.

"It's nothing any other man wouldn't do," Fargo responded.

"Don't sell yourself short. Most men wouldn't care to be seen with me in public, my being a tainted woman, and all. They'd be too afraid people would whisper behind their backs." Sally grew sad. "Yet they'll grope me in the saloon and still beg me to go to bed with them. The hypocrites."

"Forget them tonight. It's just you and me and the stars," Fargo said. Growing more confident, he spun her in a tight arc and dipped her like a winsome willow. She giggled girlishly, and when they straightened, she brazenly kissed him.

"You are so adorable."

Fargo couldn't recall the last time anyone had called him that, if ever. Ignoring the stares of a few prudish bystanders, he returned the kiss, then whisked her around the ground, flowing smoothly. The food had invigorated him. He felt more like his usual self, boiling with boundless energy.

Originally, Fargo intended to stay at the festivities just a short while. But as the evening waxed on, he lost all track of time. Sally was an excellent partner and they danced until their legs were sore. Reclaiming their seats under the tree, they watched the fireworks display. By Eastern standards it was rather puny, but the crowd cheered and clapped loudly with each dazzling burst.

Toward midnight the celebration broke up. The musicians put their instruments back in their cases. Women who had contributed dishes collected what was left of the feast. Fathers carried weary children to waiting wagons.

Under a sliver of golden moon, Fargo and Sally headed for the hotel. Sally rested her head on his wide shoulder, her hazel eyes aglow with affection.

"I honestly can't remember the last time I enjoyed myself so much. I'll be forever in your debt."

"I know how you can pay me back, if you want," Fargo said, and pinched her dainty bottom.

Sally grinned. "Men. That's all you ever think of. If all your peckers were to drop off tomorrow, the world would be a better place."

What could a man say? Fargo wisely didn't comment.

"Have you ever wondered why the Almighty made us so different? Why men have peckers and women don't?" Sally asked him.

Fargo had to admit he hadn't given it much thought.

"Well, I have. Ever since I was eighteen and saw my first naked man. About shocked me out of ten years' growth." Sally's brow knit. "The way I have it figured, men and women are like two halves of a coin. Why else would men have pokers and women have holes to poke around in? It makes for a perfect fit, don't you reckon?"

They were strolling amid high trees, in murky shadow, taking a shortcut to the street. Thanks to Sally's babbling, Fargo didn't hear the men closing in on them until they were almost on top of him. Their rush was swift, silent, deadly. Abruptly, a bulky figure materialized out of the darkness, tempered steel glittering dully in his right hand.

"We've got you now, you son of a bitch!"

Gar Myers' snarl bought Fargo the split second he needed to shove Sally Crane to safety and bound backward. The dagger cleaved the space where his throat had just been. Lunging, Gar sought to stab him in the heart but Fargo nimbly hopped out of reach. Unexpectedly, his right arm was seized by another riverman. As Fargo pivoted to throw him off, the third riverman pounced, grasping his other arm.

They had him, caught like a rabbit in a snare. All they needed to do was hold him while Gar plunged the blade into him. Gar was now advancing to do just that, showing his teeth in a wolfish grin.

"I warned you, mister. Now I'm fixing to carve you into little pieces and scatter the bits out on the prairie for the coyotes to eat."

A brunette banshee flew at Gar, her small fists flailing. "Stop it! Harm him and I'll see that you're tossed behind bars!"

"Shut up, woman." Gar backhanded Sally, cuffing her with such force she was sent sprawling.

The other two rivermen were momentarily distracted. Fargo capitalized on the moment by driving his shoulder into the one on the right, then whirling and whipping him into the riverman on the left. Fargo jerked his right arm free and used it to club the cutthroat holding his left one. The man attempted to ward him off but a solid blow rocked him back on his heels.

Fargo tore loose and vaulted aside, heartbeats ahead of Gar's dagger. Gar, hissing like a serpent, pressed at him viciously, spearing the tip repeatedly at Fargo's head and chest. Fargo had to backpedal frantically to save himself. The other two were spreading out to come at him from either side. They produced long knives of their own and crouched, preparing to rush him.

In Fargo's right boot, snug in its ankle sheath, was an Arkansas toothpick. He could wield its double-edged blade as well as any man alive. But he would be courting death to resort to it when he was so badly outnumbered. His life was at stake. So he had no qualms about doing what he did, which was to palm the Colt and trigger a shot that bored Gar's shoulder and spun the big riverman around.

As Gar crumpled, Fargo shifted. The other pair were

brought up short. "Live or die," Fargo bluntly declared. "Your choice."

They swapped looks. It was obvious which they chose.

"No hard feelings?" one asked.

"Take Myers and go," Fargo ordered. A riot of voices from the vicinity of the feast tables convinced him it wouldn't be long before the local law arrived. Backing away, he snagged Sally's wrist and raced for a side street. A lack of lanterns gave them the cover they needed, and they hastened down an alley that would bring them out almost directly across from the Yankton Imperial.

Fargo checked before venturing into the open. A loud commotion back at the knoll was proof that confusion still reined in the aftermath of his shot. But between the alley mouth and the hotel's grand double doors, all was tranquil. Draping an arm over Sally's shoulders, he whispered, "Act drunk and no one will pay any attention to us."

His hunch was right. The parson notwithstanding, many of the good people of Yankton were roaming the streets tipsy, if not worse. So two more merited no interest. As they climbed the steps to the Imperial, Fargo saw a tall lean man with a badge on his vest go racing by, his spurs jangling.

The plump desk clerk was busy polishing the counter. His frown of disapproval wasn't lost on Fargo, who guessed what he wanted before he crooked a finger at Fargo to come over.

"Wait here," Fargo told Sally.

The clerk got directly to the point. "Excuse me for saying so, sir, but your lady friend isn't permitted on the premises unless she has a room of her own."

Once again Fargo was reminded why he preferred the wide open spaces to towns and cities. "Do tell."

"Don't look at me like that. You were told the rules when you checked in. No drinking. No loud noise. And especially no women." The clerk flapped his hand at a sign on the wall that listed the three taboos. "Kindly usher her elsewhere. If you don't, I'm afraid we'll have to throw you out on your ear."

"Who's going to do the throwing? You?"

The clerk opened his mouth to reply but something in Fargo's eyes caused his Adam's apple to bob. "Please, Mr. Fargo. I don't want any trouble. I'm only doing what they pay me to do."

"How much do they pay you?"

"Sir?"

"What do you earn a month? Fifty dollars? Sixty?" Fargo suspected it was much less. Clerks, bank tellers, and stable hands weren't known for living in mansions.

"Goodness gracious, I wish it was that much."

Fargo fished out his roll of winnings and peeled off some bills. "Here's ten dollars." He was feeling generous. "A week's wages to go blind and deaf."

"Blind and—?" The clerk smiled slyly. "Oh, I understand. I'd be more than happy to accommodate you, but if my employer ever found out it would cost me my job. And my mother won't overlook the rent I owe just because I'm her own flesh and blood."

Had Fargo heard correctly? His *mother*? "Make it twenty. And I give you my word the young lady will slip out unnoticed. Do we have a deal?"

The clerk was beaming from ear to ear. "Deal." He snatched the money as if afraid Fargo would change his mind and stuffed it into a pocket. "But please get her upstairs right away! None of the other guests must know."

Fargo's room was on the third floor at the end of the hall. The window commanded a sweeping view of Yankton but at that hour there wasn't much to see. Most lamps had long since been blown out. The houses and commercial establishments were as dark as the night itself. Sally stood staring out through the parted curtains, her slender back to the room.

"Sometimes I wonder why I ever left Illinois for greener pastures. Days like this tend to remind me."

Fargo threw the bolt, dropped his hat on the dresser, removed his gunbelt, and walked up behind her. He molded his body to hers, his nose brushing her luxurious, fragrant hair. "You smell nice."

"I should. I dabbed on the most expensive perfume I own, just for you." Sally twisted her head, offering her luscious lips, which Fargo kissed without hesitation. She tasted like strawberries.

"Mmmmm, that was nice," Sally said when they parted for breath. Her cheeks were flushed and a tiny vein in her neck fluttered like a butterfly's wings. "I could go for a second helping."

Fargo turned her so they were face-to-face. He glued himself to her again, his tongue sliding into her mouth and entwining with hers. She uttered a kittenish mewl, then placed her warm hands on either side of his neck. When next they pulled away, she was breathing quite hard, her breasts heaving in the tight confines of her dress.

"Lordy. You do things to me no man has done in ages. What *is* it about you? It can't just be your good looks."

"I take baths more often than most," Fargo bantered.

Sally pealed with mirth and put a hand over her mouth to stifle it. She impishly slapped his shoulder. "If you only knew! Half the men who enter the saloon haven't bathed in a year. Why, the other day I took one whiff of a buffalo hunter and about keeled over. He was so filthy, flies were crawling over him, I swear!"

Fargo believed her. Bathing wasn't held in high esteem on the frontier. Some people, in fact, were convinced that taking a bath more than once a month was bad for one's health. But for him, few of life's joys could compare to taking a plunge in a clear mountain lake or swimming in an icy high-country stream. One of those joys that it *could* be compared to was standing in front of him, and he pulled Sally close.

Their lips met, their tongues danced. She was exquisitely soft, delightfully aromatic. Fargo rimmed her mouth as his fingers explored her shoulders, her upper arms, then angled to her breasts. Even through her dress he could feel her nipples grow taut. He tweaked first one, then the other, sparking a loud moan.

"Ohhh. This is going to be a night to remember. I just know it."

Fargo tended to agree. While kissing and licking her velvet neck and throat, he began unfastening the small gilt buttons that would grant him access to her ripe body. She leaned into him, breathing hotly into his ear, her whole body quivering. Sally craved him as much as he craved her.

Undressing her was like stripping the peel from a banana. First he unbuttoned her dress, then he had to unfasten the stays to her chemise. Much to his relief, she wasn't wearing a corset or, worse, a crinoline. Even since the collapsible hoop cages were introduced, they had been the bane of Fargo's existence. Throw in up to six petticoats, and undressing some women took forever. By the time a man got to what mattered, he'd lost interest.

Sally's dress and chemise slipped from her shoulders, revealing her glorious bosom. Her breasts were full and well-rounded, perky and firm. Her nipples, now two rigid tacks, begged to be tantalized. Fargo sucked on one, then the other, pinching them hard with his fingertips.

"Ah. Yes. Like that, handsome. Just like that."

The brunette was panting now, and she was growing weak at the knees. Fargo moved her to the bed and gently lowered her on her back. When she curled her arms over her head and formed her red lips into a teasing kiss, his pole surged upward.

"My, my. Is that what I think it is? Or do you keep a spare pistol down there?"

"See for yourself." Fargo took off his boots and spurs and stretched out beside her. Her body was giving off heat like an oven, the heat mirrored in her gaze. Her hand closed on his manhood and squeezed, and it was all he could do not to erupt like a volcano.

"A human stallion," Sally said in awe.

Fargo devoted himself to her magnificent melons. Massaging each in turn while pulling on her nipples, he soon had her squirming in anticipation. Her teeth bit lightly into his shoulder, her long nails raked his back.

"My turn." Sally undid his buckskin pants and pulled them low enough for her purpose. She cupped him, caressing him where he was most sensitive. Now it was Fargo who was groaning. She knew just what to do. When her forefinger glided to the end of his pole, he trembled like an aspen leaf.

"Like that, do you?"

"A man would have to be dead not to."

In short order Fargo got rid of the dress and the chemise and her underthings. There she lay, in all her natural beauty, his for the taking. Tucking at the waist, he kissed her ankles and then slowly worked higher, across her shins to her knees. Her thighs were as smooth as glass. They widened as his mouth continued to climb. A new fragrance tingled his nose, a new hunger filled him.

Fargo nuzzled her moist slit as Sally arched her back. She cooed and thrashed as he applied his tongue to her womanhood, her legs wrapping tight to hold him in place. Outside the window, a chill wind from the northwest blew, but in their room the temperature was rapidly rising.

"Yes! Yes! Oh, Skye!"

How long he lingered, Fargo couldn't say. She was caked with perspiration and lying limp and spent when he rose on his knees and aligned his manhood with her wet core. Sally uttered a tiny whimper as he rubbed the tip of his member against her mound.

"Now! Please do it now."

Fargo did, but slowly, ever-so-slowly, filling her, stretching her walls. Sally gripped him, her nails biting into his flesh, and locked her mouth to his. She was on fire. And so was he. Fargo plunged into her again and again, harder and harder, faster and faster. Soon she was clinging to him and making incoherent sounds. His hands gripping her bottom, he lifted her off the bed with each powerful stroke.

"Yessss! Oh, yesssss!"

Thunder seemed to boom and lightning seemed to crash as they reached the pinnacle, then crested. Fargo continued to pump his knees even as sheer bliss overcame him and he soared into an ocean of unmatchable sensation. At length they sagged against one another and drifted off to sleep.

Fargo couldn't say what awakened him. Daylight shone through the curtains and horses were clattering past the hotel. His mouth was dry, his throat parched. Smacking his lips, he sat up. Sally snored softly, beautiful in repose.

There was a light rap on the door. "Mr. Fargo? We need to talk."

Assuming it was the desk clerk, Fargo pulled on his pants and his shirt, then padded across the cold floor in his bare feet. He didn't bother with the Colt or the toothpick. He didn't think he would need them.

"Mr. Fargo?"

"Don't lay an egg," Fargo chided. Tugging on the bolt, he worked the latch and opened the door—and found himself staring down the twin barrels of a pearl-handled derringer.

3

The Weldons were back. Or two of them were, Finlay and Gordon. It was Gordon who held the Remington .41-caliber derringer. His expression left little doubt he would love for Fargo to give him any excuse to squeeze the trigger. Sighing, Fargo said, "Some people just can't take no for an answer."

"Pardon our rude manners," Finlay Weldon said, "but it's imperative we speak to you. The matter is most urgent."

Gordon was less cordial. "It's your own fault, mister. You should have heard us out yesterday."

"I didn't want to then and I don't want to now," Fargo responded with a glance at where his gunbelt lay. He couldn't possibly reach it before the hothead put two slugs into him. And his boots, with the Arkansas toothpick, were way over by the bed.

"You're not listening," Gordon said sarcastically. "You don't have any choice. Now back up, real slow, and keep your hands where I can see them."

Simmering, Fargo complied. Gordon entered first, then his brother. Both halted upon spying Sally Crane, who slept on, blissfully unaware of the intrusion.

"We should toss the slut out on her ear," Gordon said.

Finlay moved to the bed and bent low. After a moment he turned around, rested the tip of his cane on the floor, and leaned on it. "No need. She's sound asleep. We can conduct our business and be gone before she wakes."

Fargo sank into the chair. "If we have business to discuss, get it over with and get the hell out."

Gordon came closer, the derringer rock-steady in his hand. "It's like this, you frontier cretin. We're hiring you to do a job and you had better not fail."

"Go to hell." There was only so much abuse Fargo would abide. As soon as he got his hands on his pistol, he would show the pair why it wasn't healthy to go around shoving guns in others' faces.

"Why, you bas—" Gordon raised the Remington, centering it squarely on Fargo's forehead.

His brother rushed over before he could shoot. "No!" Finlay said. "How many times must Charlotte and I remind you? We need him. He's the one person who can find her. And finding her is more important than venting your petty spite." Finlay wrapped his fingers around Gordon's wrist and the latter lowered the derringer, but only a trifle.

"I'll go along with you for now," Gordon rasped. "But I don't like this guy."

"The feeling is mutual," Fargo said.

Finlay was upset. "Please, can't we start over again on the right foot? Whatever we've done to antagonize you can be remedied." He thrust out his hand. "Finlay Weldon, sir. It is an honor to make your acquaintance."

Fargo couldn't say the same but he shook the man's hand anyway. Despite himself, he was curious about why they were so desperate for his help. "What's this all about?"

"Where should I begin?" Finlay said. "I suppose it would help if you knew more about us. We're from Philadelphia. Our family is one of the oldest and most respected around, with many lucrative business interests—everything from shipping to construction. It wouldn't be an exaggeration to say that the Weldons are one of the wealthiest families in the entire country."

"And you need me to help you count all your money?" Fargo couldn't resist baiting them.

Gordon bristled. "Do you see, brother? Do you see what we have to put up with when dealing with riffraff?"

Finlay's jaw muscles twitched. "It certainly doesn't help any for you to constantly hurl insults."

"But look at him!" Gordon said. "With his decrepit buckskins and unkempt hair. *This* is the famous scout? Hell, we've seen dozens just like him. Any one of them could do what we need and they wouldn't give us half as much trouble."

"It's not the clothes, it's the man who wears them," Finlay philosophized. "Mr. Fargo has a reputation as being one of the most skilled scouts alive. Everyone of authority we've spoken with has recommended him highly. He's the best, brother, and Weldons always hire the best."

"Hire me for what?" Fargo asked.

Finlay began to walk back and forth. "We're in a bind, sir. A grave one. Unless certain steps are taken, the Weldon fortune will be lost to us. And we will take any steps necessary to ensure that doesn't occur."

"How can you lose a fortune?"

"A capricious whim of fate is to blame," Finlay said. "For generations, the family's wealth has been passed from father to sons. The last patriarch of the family, James Weldon, died about nineteen months ago. Sadly, his dear wife, who went to her own reward years ago, bore him no sons. But he did have two daughters—Charlotte, whom you've met, and her sister, Darlene, who is a couple of years older than Charlotte."

Fargo folded his hands in his lap. Something told him the explanation would take a while.

"Uncle James was forced to break with tradition. Instead of willing the fortune to his daughters, he willed them to us."

"Convenient," Fargo said.

"Not really, not when you know the whole story. Our father, a distant relative of James's, was killed in a carriage accident when we were quite young. James took us in and raised us as his own. We were just as much his sons as Charlotte and Darlene were his daughters." Finlay paused. "We never asked him to make us his heirs. But since he had made us his sons, he stuck with tradition."

"Get to the important part," Gordon said.

"Patience, brother. Patience." Finlay scowled, then went on. "There was a stipulation in his will that his daughters were to be provided for, which was fine by us. Charlotte agreed to the terms. But her sister, Darlene, opposed the will."

Fargo wasn't a legal expert but he did know a little about the law. "How could she, if the will was signed and proper?"

"It was," Finlay said. "But long ago, before James Weldon and his wife had children, he made out another will, one leaving all his wealth to his first-born, whoever that might be. Normally, the second document takes precedence over the first. But Darlene was clever. She took us to court, claiming the last will her father made out was done under duress. She asked the judge to render it void, and to legally appoint her as the rightful heir to the Weldon millions."

"The judge went along with her?"

"No, of course not. The judge was about to rule in our favor when Darlene committed a heinous act."

"She stole the second will, the one where James left everything to us," Gordon said.

Questions were piling up in Fargo's mind, but he refrained from asking them for the time being. "What good did that do her?"

"Without it, the court can't validate our claim," Finlay said. "It's the only legal proof we have. It was being kept under lock and key, but Darlene broke in somehow and made off with it."

"But they must have it on record," Fargo said.

"That's not the same as having the actual document. Believe me, no one was more surprised than I was when the attorney told us that without it, we stood to lose everything.

If only James had made additional copies . . ." Finlay shrugged.

Fargo sat up. "How do I fit in?"

"After Darlene stole the will, she fled from Philadelphia. We traced her as far as St. Louis. We almost had her, but she slipped away and booked passage on a steamboat to the frontier."

Gordon took up the account. "We were on the next steamer out. At every stop we checked, we found she had never gotten off. It wasn't until we reached Yankton that we caught up to her, and only because her steamboat has a week's layover for minor repairs. Darlene is here somewhere, in hiding."

"We want you to find her for us," Finlay said. "We're willing to pay a thousand dollars for your services."

Fargo whistled. A thousand dollars was more than many men earned in an entire year. But he failed to see where he could be of any help, and said so. "I'm a tracker, not a detective. I can find anyone on the plains or in the mountains once I pick up their trail. In a town, it's just a matter of asking around. You should pay the marshal a visit."

"We'd rather not involve the law," Finlay replied. "We don't want anyone asking around, especially not a lawman. Word would spread. Darlene would be bound to hear of it and she'd flee again."

"We want to keep this quiet," Gordon said.

Finlay nodded. "We would ask around ourselves but the same risk applies. You, on the other hand, could do so discreetly. She doesn't know you. You're not a Pinkerton or a lawman. So what do you say? Will you accept?"

A light rap on the door caused both Weldons to stiffen. Rising, Fargo walked over, conscious of the derringer trained on his back. When he saw who it was, he opened the door wide. "Looking for these two, I take it?"

Charlotte Weldon wore clothes most women could never afford. A silk dress clung to her voluptuous form, of a soft shade of pink that contrasted vividly with her striking red tresses. From atop a stiff pink hat rose a peacock feather that bobbed when she moved. In her left hand was a matching pink parasol. "So you did come," she scolded Finlay and Gordon. "After I expressly forbid it!" Charlotte marched past Fargo as if he weren't there. "I swear! Your stubbornness will jeopardize everything." She spotted Sally Crane and stopped dead.

"Time is running out," Finlay replied. "Unless we find Darlene soon, all is lost." He smiled suavely. "I've explained the situation to Mr. Fargo. We had just asked him whether he would help us when you knocked."

"You told him?" Charlotte said, sounding surprised.

"All he needs to know, yes," Finlay said.

Fargo leaned against the jamb. "My answer is the same as it was yesterday. Find someone else."

Finlay was disappointed. "Not even for the thousand dollars I offered?"

"Make it two thousand," Charlotte said. "Half now, the other half when Darlene is caught."

"That's too much," Gordon complained. "He's not worth it."

Redheads were notorious for their tempers and Charlotte Weldon was no exception. "Simpleton! Are you so cheap you wouldn't spend a couple of thousand to gain a fortune?" Her blazing green eyes narrowed. "And why are you pointing that toy of your? You've tried to persuade him at *gunpoint*?"

To Fargo's amazement, Gordon cringed. "Don't look at me like that, Charlotte. He wouldn't have heard us out otherwise. Force is the only thing these frontiersmen understand."

"Put your derringer away," the redhead commanded. "And if the two of you ever disobey me again, there will be hell to pay."

"Sorry," Gordon mumbled like a chastised child.

"Not half as sorry as I am." Charlotte faced Fargo.

"Please accept my apology on their behalf. They can be such idiots."

"Yet your father left them the family fortune? And you don't mind?" Fargo would as soon believe in fairy tales as in the yarn they had spun.

"I'm being practical," Charlotte answered. She gave her parasol a spin. "Don't misconstrue. I loved my father. Dearly. But he had his flaws, like everyone else. And one of his biggest was that in his eyes, a woman's place was in the home. Business is a man's world, he'd always say. So naturally, after he adopted Finlay and Gordon, he made them his heirs instead of my sister and me."

"And you're willing to go along with that?"

"What's done is done, Mr. Fargo. I'm mature enough to realize that. My sister, alas, isn't. She has always acted contrary to everyone else. She believes that she should be the rightful heir, and she's done all she can to sabotage the legal proceedings. Stealing the will was her final desperate gambit."

"You think she still has it? By now she's probably burned it or torn it up. Without it, won't the first will go into effect?"

"The situation is a bit more complicated than that," Charlotte said. "Suffice it to say, we only have three months left in which to find her, will or no will."

"Why is that?"

Charlotte shot Finlay a harsh look. "I thought you said that you told him everything!" Turning back to Fargo, she said, "The judge gave us six months to either produce the second will, or produce Darlene. Half that time has elapsed. If we fail, we're in danger of losing everything."

As the old saying went, something didn't quite add up. Fargo suspected they weren't telling him the whole truth. There had to be more to the legal wrangling than they were letting on. Maybe they thought he was too dumb to realize it since he was just a "frontier cretin," to use Gordon's words. On the spur of the moment Fargo said, "I'll take the job. A thousand now, a thousand when I'm done. On one condition."

"Condition?" Charlotte repeated warily.

"I work alone. I don't want anyone breathing over my shoulder. When I find her, I'll bring her to you. Fair enough?"

"More than fair." Charlotte pointed the parasol at Gordon. "You heard the man. Since you've given him the most trouble, the money should come out of your pocket. Pay him and we'll be on our way."

Gordon looked fit to gag. "Me? Why the hell should I do it? This was your crazy idea! You pay him."

Fargo had never seen any woman as furious as Charlotte Weldon now became. In two steps she reached Gordon and gouged the end of the parasol into his chest. "Did I hear you correctly? Are you defying my wishes?"

Gordon Weldon blanched. "No, no, no," he said with real fear in his voice. "I didn't mean anything. I just don't think—"

"No, you *don't* think!" Charlotte spat. "You never do. Which is why I have to do the thinking for all of us." With a visible effort she reined in her rage and lowered the parasol. In the blink of an eye her disposition changed. She turned to Fargo, smiling warmly. "Forgive him. No one has ever accused Gordon of being overly intelligent. We're staying at the Grand Hotel. Room 314. I'll expect news from you soon."

The Weldons filed out, with Charlotte in the lead. Gordon lingered just long enough to place ten one-hundred-dollar bills in Fargo's hand. "I hope you choke on it," was Gordon's parting comment.

Fargo closed and bolted the door. As he did, the blankets rustled. "So you're awake at last?" he said.

Sally Crane sat up, the sheet pulled almost to her neck. "I've been awake the whole time, handsome. I heard the whole thing. And if you ask me, you're loco for agreeing to help them out. That woman is a sidewinder."

34

"I don't trust any of them as far as I can throw a bull buf- falo," Fargo confided. Sitting on the bed, he reached for his boots.

"Then why did you accept?"

Fargo answered with a question of his own. "This Dar- lene Weldon. Have you seen her? Know of anyone who has?"

Sally's curls spilled over her shoulders in disarray, the re- sult of their passionate lovemaking the night before. She reached up to arrange them and the sheet slipped, exposing her marvelous breasts. "No, I haven't. But if she's anything like her kin, she doesn't spend much time in saloons. I can ask around for you, though."

"I'll check all the hotels," Fargo said. It was highly im- probable Darlene would stay at one unless she did so under an assumed name, but one never knew. Maybe she was as witless as Gordon.

"Do you buy that nonsense about the two wills? And Darlene stealing one of them?"

Fargo strapped the Arkansas toothpick to his ankle. "They were lying through their teeth. Why, I can't say. But I hope to find out."

"You never answered me. Why go to so much bother? Is it the money?"

"No." Fargo had won enough at poker to last him months.

"Then what?"

"I don't like having derringers shoved in my face." Fargo tugged on his right boot.

Sally laughed, her breasts jiggling. "You're doing it to spite them? What happens if you find Darlene?"

"*When* I do," Fargo amended. Now that he had set his mind to it, he wouldn't rest until he had learned what the Weldons were up to. His other boot slipped on easily.

"I just hope you're not biting off more than you can chew, lover. Money is power, folks say. Those easterners could rustle up a small army of gunmen if they wanted, more than even you could handle." Sally slid toward him.

"And I'd hate to see your wonderful body riddled with holes." Her soft lips nibbled on his ear, on his neck, on his cheek.

"Don't start anything we can't finish," Fargo cautioned.

"Who says we can't? I'm not due at work until noon."

They kissed. Sally's mouth widened to receive Fargo's tongue as her fingers plucked at his pants. He felt himself swell, hardening at her touch. So did she, and she grinned mischievously.

"My, my. And here I was worried that I'd worn you out last night. I guess it's true—you can't keep a good man down."

There was none of the prolonged foreplay of the night before. Fargo pulled her close, and pulled her leg over his so she could straddle his waist. A nipple filled his vision and he enfolded it in his mouth, rubbing it with his tongue.

"Mmmm. Now this is the right way to start a day," Sally teased. She opened his pants and gripped his pole. "You agree, I take it?"

Fargo slid a hand between her thighs, ensured his manhood was angled just right, then drove up into her as if impaling her on a lance. Sally threw back her head and gasped. Her hips began to move of their own accord as he commenced a regular rhythm of powerful strokes.

"Oh. Oh. I'm so hot for you."

Fargo could tell. Her womanhood fit him like a scabbard fit a sword. Each upward surge seemed to cleave her in two, her inner walls rippling against his hard flesh. Gripping her waist, he pounded into her again and again and again. Sally began puffing like someone who had run a mile, her eyes closed, her lips drawn back in a rapturous smile.

The bed started bouncing up and down, thumping loudly and growing louder the faster their pace became. Sally's low moans rose in volume as her enjoyment mounted. Fargo kneaded her breasts, her back, her thighs.

"It shouldn't be long," Sally cooed.

It wasn't, not for her. She suddenly gripped Fargo's shoulders, cried out, and burst into a violent fit of pumping, her body shaking uncontrollably, the tip of her tongue swirling around and around her lips.

"Yes! Oh, Lord, yes!"

She was in for a surprise. Fargo wasn't ready yet. After Sally calmed and slowly coasted to a weary stop, he resumed levering himself upward. Eyes widening, she gasped, then grinned.

"I sure can pick 'em," she breathed.

Fargo paced himself. The bed shook and rattled as if on the verge of falling apart. The creaking and thumping were bound to be heard by anyone in adjoining rooms but Fargo didn't care. They rose and fell as if in a canoe on choppy waters. It went on and on, Sally sagging against him, lost in sexual delirium. A tight sensation in his groin eventually signaled his release. He gushed like a geyser, holding her tight, while she groaned his name over and over.

Slumping onto the bed, they lay snuggled together until another knock on the door roused Fargo. Putting his buckskins in order, he strapped on his gunbelt before opening the door. A mousey man in a striped suit, whom Fargo recognized as the day clerk, was impatiently rocking on his heels.

"Mr. Fargo? Awful sorry to disturb you. But Mrs. Hoffmeyer, who has the room under yours, claims she heard unseemly sounds coming from your room a while ago."

"Unseemly sounds?"

The clerk coughed and reddened. "You know. Sounds a man and woman make when—" he broke off and squared his slim shoulders. "Do you have a woman in there with you? I hope not. It's against the rules."

"I know."

"I'm afraid I'll have to take a look for myself," the clerk said.

Fargo debated bribing him just as he had the night clerk. A glance back changed his mind. "Be my guest." Grinning, he stepped aside so the clerk could enter. "What was your name, again?"

"Charlie Thompson. I was on duty when you signed—" Charlie entered, then froze. As well he should.

By the bed stood Sally Crane, as naked as the day she was born. She pretended to be shocked and grabbed the top blanket. "My word! What is this world coming to when a woman can't dress in private?"

"You do have a woman in here!" Charlie exclaimed, flabbergasted.

"Well, I'm sure not a squirrel," Sally retorted. "And I'll thank you to avert your eyes, you pervert. Wait until the management hears of this!"

Charlie's mouth was hanging down around his waist. "M-m-management?" he stuttered. "But you're the one in the wrong."

Sally had wrapped the blanket around herself so that the tops of her breasts and most of her right leg were exposed. "What's wrong with visiting my brother?"

"B-b-brother?" Charlie stammered, unable to take his eyes off all her bare skin.

"What did *you* think was going on?" Sally asked sweetly. Sashaying up to him, she patted his cheek as if he were a puppy. "My, aren't you cute. How would you like to be my escort tonight?"

"E-e-escort?"

"Meet me in front of the dry-goods store on Second Street at seven. You can show me the sights."

"Me? You want a date with me?" Charlie touched his cheek in awe. "This can't be happening."

Sally clasped his hand. "Of course it can. Now you run along and let me finish dressing. And don't forget. Second Street at seven."

"Second Street," the clerk said, his legs now spongy. "I'll be there. I promise. And I'll bring flowers and everything."

"You do that, cute boy." Sally pushed him out the door and closed it. She pressed an ear to the panel, then announced, "He's gone!" Doubling over, she shared a belly laugh with Fargo. It was a full minute before they composed themselves.

"I'm your brother?" Fargo said.

"Thank your other visitors. They gave me the brainstorm, the way they were calling each other 'brother' and all." Sally padded toward her dress. "Now you'd better smuggle me out the back way pronto, before that clerk comes to his senses."

Fargo absently nodded. He was already thinking about the chore he had set for himself—finding Darlene Weldon.

4

It turned out to be a lot more difficult than Skye Fargo
reckoned. Yankton wasn't all that big, but finding Darlene
Weldon was a lot like looking for the proverbial needle in a
haystack. For one thing, the celebration had drawn folks
from far and wide, swelling the town's usual population by
several hundred. For another, there were the steamboats
that routinely berthed at Yankton, sometimes nine or ten at
a time.

The result was that women, once scarce on the frontier
and as rare as gold in Yankton, had become a common
sight. Fargo had his hands full checking every hotel and
trying to find out how many other establishments and private homes rented rooms. It didn't help that he had ne-
glected to ask for a description of Darlene. Nor that she had
undoubtedly changed her name.

Shortly after noon Fargo bent his steps to the Grand
Hotel. Like the Imperial, it didn't offer the luxurious ac-
commodations its name implied. Each room had a bed, a
chair, and a dresser. And that was it. People willing to pay
a little more were entitled to a bath in one of the tubs in a
back room. Maid service was weekly. And even when the
windows were kept shut tight, dust seeped in, caking everything.

Fargo strode into the Grand's lobby and was surprised to
see the same plump clerk from the Imperial he had bribed
the night before. The man was registering a pair of elderly
guests and didn't see Fargo until he stepped to the counter.

"You?" The clerk went rigid, his mouth working like that of a fish out of water. "What are you doing here?"

"I could ask you the same."

Glancing both ways, the clerk leaned toward him. "Keep this between us, will you? To make ends meet I hold two jobs. Neither employer knows about the other, and I'd like to keep it that way. They might fire me if they knew I was working for a competitor."

"How much are you willing to pay me to keep quiet?" Fargo joked. But the clerk gripped the edge of the counter and reeled as if he were about to faint. "Relax. It's no concern of mine."

"Oh." The man gulped, then exhaled. "Thank goodness. I used that money you gave me to pay my mother the rent money I owed."

"Ever thought of moving out on your own?"

"Why should I? My mother provides all my meals and does my laundry. That would cost extra elsewhere. Living at home is cozy. The only drawback is that she won't let me bring any girls around, but who needs 'em anyhow?"

"Were you stomped on the head by a horse when you were little?"

"No. Why on earth would you ask such a thing?"

"No reason." In Fargo's travels he had met some strange people. He mentally added the clerk to the list. "Are the Weldons in their room?"

"I can't honestly say. I know they were in earlier, but they might have gone out and I didn't notice. We've been pretty busy this morning."

"Much obliged." Fargo took the stairs two at a time. The third floor was deserted. He knocked once on 314 and the door was immediately opened by the dazzling redhead. She wore a different silk dress, a blue one, that clung to her figure in all the right places.

"Mr. Fargo. To what do I owe this honor?" Charlotte Weldon motioned to him. "Come in, why don't you?"

No one else was present in the room. Fargo doffed his

hat as she glided to a chair, her dress rustling softly, her long legs accented by the clinging material. "Where are Finlay and Gordon?"

"They have the next room over," Charlotte answered. "I'm not about to share one with them. They never pick up after themselves, and Gordon snores loud enough to wake the dead." Her keen green eyes appraised him intently. "Is this a social visit, or have you found my sister?"

"I need to know what she looks like."

"An oversight on my part. I should have thought of it yesterday." Charlotte rose and stepped to a traveling bag on the dresser. "I can do better than describe her. I can show you a photograph taken about three years ago."

The whole room had a flowery scent that grew stronger as Charlotte drew near. She was an exceptionally attractive woman, her mane of red hair gleaming in the shafts of sunlight that pierced the window. Yet there was a cold, calculating quality about her that detracted from her beauty. Fargo had seen it in her eyes the previous night, and he saw it now as she brusquely handed him the photograph.

"As you can see, we're little alike. Which has made me suspect that my mother might have had a dalliance or two in her day."

The photo showed a smiling young woman with long hair and gleaming eyes. White, even teeth, a button nose and high cheekbones completed the picture. Darlene was every bit as lovely as Charlotte and radiated a quality her sister lacked. Genuine warmth shone in her expression and her smile.

"She has blond hair and blue eyes," informed Darlene.

"She's beautiful," Fargo said to see what sort of reaction he would get.

"And I'm not?" Charlotte's rosy mouth quirked. "I'll have you know men usually fall over themselves to please me." Her eyes narrowed. "But not you, I've noticed. Why is that, Mr. Fargo? What makes you immune to my charms?"

"Who said I am?" Fargo countered.

Charlotte inched so close, her bosom almost touched his chest. A twinkle came into her eyes and she grinned. "Thank you for restoring my confidence. You're rather good-looking, too, in a rough-hewn sort of way. Play your cards right, as they say in your parlance, and you might be rewarded for your efforts with more than just money."

"Is that so?" Fargo grabbed her around the waist and pulled her to him, fusing his mouth to hers. She instantly stiffened and pushed back.

Charlotte was as red as her hair. Her fists were balled and her bosom heaving with indignation. "How dare you! What presumption! I said that *after* your job is done you *might* be entitled to a night in my arms! Take a liberty like that again and I'll scratch your eyes out."

Smirking, Fargo moved to the door. "I just wanted to see if you were worth spending a night with. The way you kiss, I'd enjoy myself more with a fish."

To say Charlotte Weldon was incensed didn't do her justice. She started toward him, then stopped, shaking with rage. "You miserable lout. I would kill you where you stand if we didn't need you."

Fargo believed her, and it gave him cause to wonder. "Can I take the photograph with me?" he asked.

Though flustered, Charlotte acted bewildered by his behavior. "The photo? Yes. Go ahead. But return it in one piece."

Tucking it under his shirt, Fargo reached for the latch. "I'll let you know as soon as I learn anything." Her eyes felt like twin barbs in his back as he left and descended to the lobby. He was halfway to the entrance when the desk clerk called his name.

"They were just here but they went right back out."

"Who was?" Fargo had no idea what this momma's boy was talking about.

"Finlay and Gordon Weldon. They came in right after you did and asked if I knew why you were here. I told them you were looking for them, but they left again. The short one, Gordon, threatened to punch my teeth in if I told you." The clerk smiled. "He can go jump in the Missouri, for all I care. You've been right friendly to me."

Fargo walked to the counter and produced the thousand dollars the Weldons had paid him. He handed a hundred-dollar bill to the astounded clerk.

"What on earth is this for? I didn't ask for any money."

"When is your next day off?"

"My what?" The clerk was stupefied. "Um, let me think. Not until the end of the month. Why?"

"I want you to save the hundred. On your day off, late in the afternoon, go to the Lucky Dollar Saloon. Ask for Sally Crane. Tell her I sent you. Then show her a good time with that hundred." Fargo shoved the money back into his pocket and strolled off.

"Wait! I don't understand!"

"You will."

Outside, Fargo squinted in the bright glare, scanning the street. Riders and wagons passed to and fro. People on foot were going about their business, a steady stream of towns-men, farmers, rivermen, and more. He saw a few soldiers laughing and joking, a few friendly Pawnees, and several dogs. But not the pair he was looking for.

Fargo turned left. At the next junction he headed south, toward the river. He took his time, stopping often to stare into stores. It wasn't their wares that interested him—it was the reflection in their glass windows. He hadn't gone far when he spotted the dandies in the reflection of a cafe's window.

Finlay and Gordon were following him. They were trying to be secretive about it but they were as stealthy as blind buffalo. They poked their heads around corners and darted from cover to cover like schoolboys playing hide-and-seek.

Fargo made for the levee. Eight steamboats were tied up to the landing. One was unloading passengers, while another was taking on a load of wood to fuel the next leg of its journey. A crowd had gathered, as was always the case when a new steamer arrived.

Pretending to be interested in the goings-on, Fargo slowly drifted toward the end of the levee, where recently unloaded cargo was awaiting transport. Hundreds of crates and barrels had been piled high in haphazard rows, creating a maze.

Only a few workers were on hand and none objected when Fargo strolled down one of the tows. As soon as he turned a corner, he broke into a run, seeking the ideal spot for what he had in mind. A stack of pallets six feet high served his purpose. He quickly climbed to the top and flattened himself down.

It wasn't long before he heard thudding footsteps, and into view jogged Finlay and Gordon. They looked worried, and had thrown caution aside.

"Where can he be?" Gordon was saying.

"He has to be here somewhere," Finlay responded. "We saw him come his way."

Gordon slowed as they neared a bend just past the pallets. "We'd best not lose him, brother, or Charlotte will have our heads."

The Weldons halted and Gordon peeked past a pillar of crates. "Damn. I don't see him. Where the hell is he?"

Quietly, Fargo rose. As they started forward he coiled and jumped. Whirling, Finlay gripped the ivory handle of his cane while Gordon darted a hand under his jacket. Fargo's Colt was out and cocked before either could produce a weapon. "Put your arms in the air," he directed.

Finlay obeyed but Gordon balked, his hand still under his jacket.

"Are you that anxious to die?" Fargo asked.

Swearing, Gordon jerked his arms up. "What's the meaning of this, you yack? You're working for us, remember?"

Fargo sincerely wished the hothead had tried to unlimber

the Remington. "Why does Charlotte have you shadowing me? Doesn't she trust me?"

"Sweet Charlotte has the disposition of a viper," Finlay said. "She doesn't trust anyone. That includes my brother and me. And it most certainly includes you." He didn't seem any happier about it than Fargo. "She sent us to keep an eye on you. She wants to know the instant you find her sister."

"What makes her so confident I will?"

"Don't be so modest, Mr. Fargo," Finlay said. "At Fort Leavenworth we were told by none other than the commanding officer that the U.S. Army holds you in the highest respect. The best scout on the Plains, was how he described you. As trustworthy as can be. When you're given a job, you always complete it."

The information intrigued Fargo. It showed that the Weldons had been asking around for someone to help them long before they arrived in Yankton. "There are a lot of other scouts who are just as good," he said.

"Perhaps. We met a few, but Charlotte wasn't impressed by them. When we heard you were here, she set her mind on hiring you. And once Charlotte makes up her mind, neither heaven nor hell can change it."

"You can lower your arms." Fargo returned the pistol to its holster with a deft reverse twirl. "Tell Charlotte I don't like being shadowed. And that if I see either of you following me again, I'll quit."

Gordon's belligerence quickly surfaced. "You can't! We paid you a thousand dollars in advance. You have to see it through."

"You're west of the Mississippi now," Fargo reminded him. "Out here a man can do as he damn well pleases. But just to show I'm not the bastard you are, I'll give back most of the money if I decide not to earn it."

"I'll kill you," Gordon simply stated.

Finlay glared at his brother. "Quit wagging that acid

tongue of yours. Or would you rather try and explain to Charlotte how your pigheadedness turned him against us?"

The taller brother had it all wrong. Fargo had taken an instinctive dislike to both of them the moment he met them, but he saw no reason to say so. Since they weren't quite as tight-lipped as Charlotte, he took advantage of the opportunity to ask, "Tell me more about Darlene. What kind of woman is she? What sort of things does she like to do?"

"What difference does that make?" Gordon asked.

"It might help me track her down."

Finlay, ever the levelheaded one, leaned on his cane, as was his habit, then said, "Darlene is the opposite of Charlotte. You can't imagine sisters who are less alike. When they were girls, Darlene was always going around with her head in the clouds. She liked to read, to recite poetry, to fritter away the hours swinging on a swing or taking long strolls around a lake on the estate. Charlotte was all business, always at her father's elbow, helping him run his financial empire."

"Yet he left his fortune to you and your brother?"

"You're suspicious. I don't blame you. I'd be, too, in your shoes. But as much as James loved Charlotte, he refused to sign his business over to a woman. Surely you've met men like him before?"

Regrettably, Fargo had. They were all too common, men who believed females were inferior. They were fools. Women were every bit as smart as any man. And Fargo had met some who could shoot and ride and live off the land as well as anyone. He held women in the highest regard and had no respect for those who didn't.

"Once the court has ruled in our favor, I intend to appoint Charlotte to the position she deserves," Finlay was saying. "She'll do all the work and I'll reap the benefits. I'm no businessman myself, but I'm shrewd enough to know the Weldon empire will crumble without her strong leadership."

Fargo saw Gordon roll his eyes skyward. "You don't agree?"

"Whatever my brother says is Gospel as far as I'm concerned," the hothead lied. "Charlotte has our best interests at heart. Anything she wants, we're glad to do."

"Tell me more about Darlene," Fargo prompted.

"There isn't much else," Finlay said. "She's fond of animals and small children. She likes to ride. And at night she'll sit up gazing at the stars for hours on end."

"A real nut," Gordon said.

The portrait they painted didn't strike Fargo as that of a greedy woman so hungry for her father's fortune, who would steal his will and flee to the frontier. "Did she have any suitors?"

Finlay adjusted his high hat. "A few beans, as I recall. Dreamers who fancied themselves poets. And a professor at a local university—a music instructor, I believe he was. He was teaching her the piano and they fell in love."

"What happened?" Fargo inquired.

Gordon snickered. "Her father found out and forbid her to see him. When she refused to listen, he had some men pay the professor a visit. Next we heard, the professor had left for parts unknown. James ruled his roost with an iron fist."

"Were either of you close to Darlene?"

"Not on your life," Gordon said. "She didn't want anything to do with me. I was always nice to her, too."

Somehow, Fargo couldn't envision Gordon being nice to *anyone*.

Finlay gave more details. "Darlene could never accept the fact that her father favored us over her. She resented it when James adopted us. For years she tried to convince him not to include us in his will. And each time he refused, it made her madder. It reached the point where she wouldn't even speak to either of us."

"You should have seen her in the courtroom," Gordon

said. "Ranting and raving about how we were swindlers and she should be the rightful heir."

Finlay's mouth pinched tight. "I think we've told Mr. Fargo more than enough. Now he can continue his search while we report back to Charlotte." He walked off, saying over a shoulder, "We're counting on you, Mr. Fargo, to do what's right. Don't disappoint us."

"Or else," Gordon added.

Fargo had a lot to mull over as he threaded through the cargo to a side street that eventually brought him to Broadway. He passed a judge's log house and the meat market, so deep in thought that he didn't hear his name being called until Sally Crane was halfway across the street.

"There you are! I've been looking all over for you." She clasped his hand and held it against her bosom.

"Not now," Fargo said. "I'm busy." He'd always been amused by the fact that women liked to claim men could never get enough of their wares. Yet, were the truth to be known, women were every bit as hungry for sexual delights. In some instances, even more so.

"Typical," Sally said, and laughed. "Here I try to do you a favor, and all you think I'm interested in is getting you under the sheets again."

Fargo waited for her to explain.

"I've lived in Yankton over a year, and I know a few of the ladies who rent out rooms in their homes. One is a sassy old gal named Flora. None of her neighbors know it, but Flora used to be a soiled dove, just like me. She scrimped and saved to buy her own house, and now she makes ends meet by renting out four or five rooms."

"And?"

"Flora hasn't taken in any new boarders in a while. But she says there's a woman who lives out at the north end of town, a friend of hers named Amanda Plumber, who took in a young easterner about three days ago when the *Altoona II* docked." Sally took a strip of paper from her purse. "I jotted down the address for you."

Fargo smiled. "I'm in your debt."

"Guess how I want to be repaid?" Sally snickered and glanced leeringly at his crotch. "You know where to find me." Kissing his chin, she pivoted and ambled away, every male she passed openly ogling her.

Lady Luck was smiling on him, Fargo reflected. He hurried northward after scouring Broadway for sign of the two brothers. Amanda Plumber's place was on Yankton's outskirts; only two other houses were further out. A picket fence and a small flower bed lent it a quaint air. It had recently been painted bright yellow. Blade shutters framed the windows.

Opening the gate, Fargo walked down a gravel path to the porch. He had just lifted a boot onto the house's steps when the door opened and out lumbered a veritable walking wall—a bearded behemoth in a soiled cotton shirt and overalls. He planted himself, his large hands wrapped around his suspenders.

"You want something, mister?"

"Amanda Plumber," Fargo said.

"My sister is busy. If it's a room you're after, she only rents to women. Safer that way." The behemoth assumed that had settled the issue and turned to go back in.

"I'm not after a room. I'm looking for someone." Fargo dug the photograph out and extended it. "Is she here?"

The man blinked. Plainly, he knew her, but he adopted an innocent air and said, "Never saw the lady before. So off you go."

Fargo didn't budge. "I'd like to talk to Amanda."

"Are your ears plugged with wax? My sister can't be bothered. And the lady you're after isn't staying here." The man lowered his massive arms. "Unless you want me to break you over my knee, you'll scat."

"I'm not leaving."

The air crackled with tension. Fargo was sure this slab of muscle would jump him. But through the doorway flitted a homely wisp of a woman in a homespun dress, who grabbed the man's forearm before he could pounce on the Trailsman.

"No violence, Horace. It might upset our boarders." She moved in front of him. "I'm Amanda Plumber. What's this all about?"

"Her," Fargo said, holding the photograph up. "Darlene Weldon. It's very important I see her."

"No one by that name is staying here."

Fargo was tired of being lied to. But to call Amanda a liar to her face would anger Horace, who looked as if he were strong enough to hoist an anvil in one arm and a keelboat in the other. "My mistake," Fargo said, smiling and backing away. He went out the gate, closed it, and ambled off down the street. Not until he veered onto another street, bearing west, did he glance over his shoulder.

The Plumbers were nowhere to be seen and their front door was closed. A curtain on the first floor moved. Fargo glimpsed a face, but the distance was too great to tell who it was.

At the next intersection Fargo turned north again. The Plumber house soon reappeared, a hundred yards east of where he was. He continued north, out past the last of the homes on the town's outskirts, traveling in a wide loop that brought him to the rear of the Plumber place five minutes later.

Propping a hand on the top rail of the picket fence, Fargo vaulted over. He landed lightly and darted to a woodshed.

The back of the house was bathed in sunshine. Through a window, a kitchen stove and a table were visible. There was no movement, which was encouraging. Hoping the Plumbers were in one of the front rooms, Fargo scooted across the yard and ducked low to pass under the kitchen window. At the stairs, he paused to listen. Somewhere above a woman was humming. From the front of the house came muffled voices.

Short wooden steps led to the back door. As soon as Fargo put his boot on the bottom one, it creaked like a rusty hinge, and he immediately stiffened. The humming and the voices never stopped, so he climbed to the top step and gingerly tried the knob.

The door was locked.

Undeterred, Fargo hopped down to the ground and over to the kitchen window. Peering in, he verified no one was around. Then he pushed up on the lowest sash bar. For a moment the window resisted, and he thought it must be latched, but then it became unstuck and it slid partway open.

Fargo grinned. On the other side of the tidy kitchen were stairs leading up to the rented rooms. If he was quiet enough, he could sneak upstairs and find Darlene, with the Plumbers being none the wiser. He raised the window as far as it would go, gripped the apron, and began to lever himself inside.

Out of nowhere an iron vise clamped onto Fargo's right shoulder and he was ripped loose and flung outside to the earth so brutally he thought his spine cracked. The world spun and flickered. Seconds later, when his vision cleared, he was lying at the foot of the huge man, whose bearded head seemed to brush the clouds.

Horace Plumber wasn't pleased to see him. "You shouldn't have come back, mister. Now I'm going to bust you into a million pieces."

5

Years of practice had made Skye Fargo lightning fast on the draw. If he'd wanted to, he could whip out his Colt and put three slugs into Horace Plumber before Plumber laid another finger on him. But Fargo couldn't bring himself to gun down an unarmed man, especially one who was only defending his home and those in it. Although Fargo's hand streaked to his pistol, he hesitated, and his moment of indecision proved costly.

Horace Plumber wrapped fingers as thick as railroad ties around Fargo's buckskin shirt and heaved him up off the ground effortlessly; as if Fargo were a child's rag doll. Horace shook Fargo like a grizzly shaking a marmot, declaring, "This won't be pleasant, mister. You might want to close your eyes."

Fargo couldn't respond. He had to grit his teeth to prevent them from snapping together every time Plumber shook him. He tried to kick at Horace but the ground suddenly changed positions with the sky and he was flung like a sack of potatoes. Air whisked past his ears. When Fargo hit, it felt as if every bone in his body had shattered. Everything went black as he struggled to breathe.

"I told you," Horace's voice boomed hollowly. "You shouldn't have gotten me riled. You should have left well enough alone."

Fargo was inclined to agree. "Listen—" he croaked, but Plumber wasn't listening. Horace seized him again and lifted him high overhead. "Don't!" Fargo yelled.

Horace did. Fargo flew end over end, his limbs flapping like those of an ungainly crow. The next impact wasn't quite as jarring as the first, but left him stunned just the same, the sky spinning like a top high overhead. He was queasy, his legs like mush.

Again the man-mountain reared over him. Despite the thrashing he was doling out Horace showed no spite, no ill-will. "I have a duty to my sister and the ladies who stay here, mister. I have to protect them from sneaky fellas like you."

"I'm not here to hurt anyone," Fargo got out before he was gripped by the shirt once more. He decided enough was enough. Horace was in the right, but that didn't mean Fargo had to stand still for being battered to a pulp. "Let me down and we can talk this out."

"Not on your life."

That did it. Fargo rammed his left fist against Horace's forehead. It was like punching a log. Horace grunted, almost losing his hold, then dug his fingers in deeper.

"You shouldn't ought to have done that."

Fargo struck out again as Horace lumbered forward, rapidly gaining speed. Ahead was the woodshed. Divining what the man was up to, Fargo thrashed and kicked, desperately seeking to break free.

"This is going to hurt you awful," Horace said.

There was no doubt about that. Fargo was hurled at the side of the shed. He attempted to twist in midair so his back bore the brunt of the fall, but he wasn't entirely successful. He crashed into the shed wall like a human cannonball. Wood splintered under the impact and he tumbled, lanced with pain. The next thing he knew, he was lying on his side inside the musty shed, with hundreds of dust motes hanging in the air around him. Horace's granite visage appeared in the gaping hole in the wall made by Fargo's flying body.

"Anything broken, mister?"

It didn't feel as if anything were. By some miracle, Fargo had been spared serious injury. He tested his arms and legs as he slowly sat up. Other than an ache in his left side, he was fine. "I'm still in one piece," he marveled.

"Learned your lesson yet?" Horace reached through the hole, his enormous arms bulging at his shirt-sleeve, as he gripped Fargo's shirt. "If not, I can keep this up for a month of Sundays."

"You're making a mistake."

"Wrong. You're the one who made the mistake by not staying away. Miss Cooper said she doesn't want to be bothered by anyone."

"Cooper—?" Fargo asked, then realized that must be the name Darlene Weldon was currently using. Placing his hands flat on either side of the hole, he resisted being pulled out. "If you'd just show her the photograph, we can settle this. Tell her I'm not out to do her any harm."

Horace clucked some more. "The pretty lady asked me real nice to keep visitors away. And that's exactly what I aim to do." Applying more of his prodigious strength, he began to drag Fargo out. "She's a real sweet lady, mister. She always smiles and treats me decent. I'm not letting anyone bother her."

"But she's in trouble—" Fargo started to explain.

"No. You are."

Fargo was yanked from the woodshed and held by the neck. Thick thumbs gouged into his throat, pressing into his windpipe.

"Ever been throttled, mister?"

The pressure was too great for Fargo to answer, even if he wanted to. He bashed his fists against Horace's forearms but it was like striking stout tree limbs. The man was solid muscle. He had no weaknesses, none at all. The thought gave Fargo a start. *Every* man had a weakness. The same weakness. Big or small, it was of no consequence. By virtue of their birth, they all had one soft spot. Marshaling his energy, Fargo arced his feet backward, then drove them into Horace Plumber's groin.

For a few seconds it seemed as if Horace was as impervious below the belt as he was above it. Then Horace's face began to change color, first a reddish tint which soon darkened into a deep purple. His eyes crossed, his mouth gaped, and his knees buckled.

As Horace's fingers slackened, Fargo wrenched to the left. Dropping to his hands and knees, he immediately scrambled upright, palming the Colt. He would be damned if he would let the man throw him again. "I only want to talk to the woman. Can't you get that through your thick skull?"

"Put the six-shooter away or I'll blow you in half."

The command came from the back steps. Fargo whirled. Amanda Plumber had him covered with a double-barreled shotgun. Both hammers had been pulled back. All it would take was the slightest of taps on the twin triggers and she would make good on her threat.

"Don't do anything I'll regret," Fargo said, carefully replacing the revolver.

Amanda glanced at the hole in the woodshed, then at her brother. "Horace, I love you, but sometimes you vex me. I saw it all, and there was no need for you to treat this jasper the way you did."

The purple was slowly fading from Horace's face, but he was still doubled over. "I was only protecting Miss Cooper," he muttered glumly.

"I know, you lovable lummox." Amanda grew stern and tucked the shotgun's stock to her shoulder. "As for you, stranger, I'd light a shuck, were I you, before this accidentally goes off. There won't be enough of you left to scrape up with a spoon."

They had a saying in Texas, "Buckshot means burying." Fargo wasn't about to rile a testy female holding a shotgun. "I'll go, but only if you'll do me a favor."

"You're in no position to make demands."

"All I'm asking is for you to tell the woman you know as Miss Cooper that I was here, and that I'd like to meet her.

Tell her it's important. It concerns her sister and her step-brothers. She'll understand."

"I'm not making any promises," Amanda said. "But if I do, how will she get word to you?"

"Send your brother with a note to the Imperial Hotel."

A new voice interjected, low and melodious. "That won't be necessary. Whatever we need to discuss can be done here and now."

Framed in the doorway was the object of all the fuss. Her photograph had shown she was beautiful, but the photo didn't begin to do Darlene Weldon justice. Her golden hair shone like the sun, her features were flawless, her body as superb as Sally Crane's. A light green dress with a high collar and long sleeves wrapped around her like a second skin. She came out and laid a hand on Amanda Plumber's shoulder. "Thank you for protecting me."

"You sure about this?" Amanda asked.

"It was bound to happen sooner or later," Darlene said. She walked down the steps and over to Horace, who was unfurling but still flushed. She touched his cheek and he grinned like a boy given a handful of hard candy. "I thank you, too, dear Horace. It was very noble of you. But I'd rather perish than have you suffer on my behalf."

"I can still make him leave," Horace croaked.

"No. Go inside. I'll be fine."

Horace was loath to leave. Eyeing Fargo as if he were a rabid wolf, Horace shuffled toward the house. "If he so much as lifts a finger against you, give a holler, Miss Cooper, and I'll come a-running."

Fargo didn't breathe easy until Amanda had let down the hammers on the shotgun. She marched indoors in her brother's wake, making a point of looking at Fargo and patting the shotgun as she went in. The threat was clear. "Are you paying them extra to be your bodyguards?" he asked in jest.

Darlene took him seriously. "No. They're doing it on their own. The Plumbers are incredibly kind, decent people.

I'm fortunate to have met them." Straightening, she roved her gaze over him from head to toe. "It's unlikely I can say the same about you."

"You don't even know me."

"No, but if my sister sent you, then I can guess the kind of man you are. Some scoundrel she found wandering the streets and paid to hunt me down. Now you'll report back to her that you've found me and my nightmare will begin all over again."

A great sadness afflicted her. Fargo was quick to say, "It's not what you think. Yes, Charlotte hired me. But whether I tell her I found you is up to me."

Darlene's sparkling blue eyes betrayed rising contempt. "Ah. I see. Playing us against one another, is that it? You'll keep quiet if I pay you more than she did?"

"Don't jump to conclusions," Fargo said. Her beauty and quiet bearing were having an effect. She wasn't anything like her sister claimed. "I'm not doing this for the money."

"Then why?" Darlene was skeptical, and rightfully so. She glanced toward the street as if fearing he wasn't alone.

"I don't want anything to happen to you."

Darlene was startled. "What do you take me for? Why should you care what happens? We've never met before. I'm nothing to you."

Beside the woodshed was a rickety bench. "Mind if we sit?" Fargo said, and plunked himself down. His left leg was aching him. Hiking his pants, he discovered a gash on his shin, the result of being thrown through the wall. "Your friend Horace doesn't know his own strength."

Cautiously, Darlene moved to the other end of the bench and sat with her hands folded in her lap. "I'm truly sorry." She locked eyes with him. "What do you really want? What is this all about, Mr.—?"

"Fargo," he introduced himself, removing his hat. "I've heard your sister's side of the story. Now I'd like to hear yours."

"What *is* her side? What are the lies she's telling about me?"

Fargo recited a brief account. "According to Charlotte, Finlay, and Gordon, all they want is the will you stole, the one your father made out appointing Finlay and Gordon as the rightful heirs."

Darlene had listened attentively. She wasn't quite as tense as before, but her fingers wouldn't stop twining and untwining. "Am I to gather you don't believe them? Why should that be?"

"Because I didn't fall out of the sky with the last rain," Fargo said. "I've met people like your sister before, people who use others to get what they want, then stab them in the back."

"You certainly have Charlotte pegged," Darlene said. "Ever since we were children she's been cold and calculating. She'll do positively anything to get what she wants. As our father learned to his misfortune."

"Tell me more. I wasn't lying to you. I'd honestly like to help." Without thinking, Fargo reached for her hand to squeeze it but she recoiled as if he were a snake about to bite her. "Sorry."

"I'm the one who should apologize," Darlene said softly. "There was a time when I trusted everyone. When I thought that no human being could possibly harm another." She bit her lower lip. "I was so naive. So gullible."

Fargo spied Amanda peering at them from the kitchen window. "We all do foolish things when we're young."

"True. But I should have known better. I was too much the idealist."

"You loved poetry, I hear."

"Charlotte told you *that*?" Darlene was incredulous. "Yes, I whiled away the days lost in poetry books or composing poems of my own. I filled reams of paper with my scribbling. It was my dream to one day be a famous poetess."

"Nothing wrong with that," Fargo remarked.

"There is if you let your passion for an ideal blind you to reality. While I was frittering my life away, my sister was plotting to take control of the Weldon empire."

Fargo smiled over at Amanda to demonstrate he was harmless. She held the shotgun up for him to see.

"Charlotte always hated me," Darlene said. "Why, I don't know." Her eyes moistened. "When we were little our father often gave us gifts. If she liked mine better than hers and I wouldn't give it to her, it would mysteriously disappear or I would find it broken. I never realized the depth of her hatred until much later, though. She is ruthless, Mr. Fargo. Charlotte will cut down anyone who stands in her way—even me."

In a bush in the middle of the yard, a sparrow was chirping and Darlene stopped until it was done. "Hear that? So carefree, so full of life." She sighed. "Charlotte has told you a pack of lies, I'm afraid. Yes, it's true that I stole the will. But there is only *one* will, not two, and in it my father left our family's fortune to me, not to her or my adoptive brothers."

"Then why are you running?"

"Because I don't want to die, Mr. Fargo." A tear trickled down Darlene's left cheek.

"Your sister has threatened to kill you?"

"She's done more than threaten. Twice she tried to have me murdered—once in Philadelphia and once in St. Louis. Each time I barely escaped with my life. My hope was to elude her, to hide for a while and go back when she gave up the search. But I've been deceiving myself. Charlotte won't give up until I'm dead and she is appointed the sole heir."

"How can she be? Your father left everything to you," Fargo said, needing to learn as much as he could.

"That's why she wants me dead. In the will, it says that if I die, everything falls into her hands. Not to Finlay and Gordon." Darlene brushed away the tear. "The truth in a nutshell is that after my father died, Charlotte took me to court to dispute the will. She tried to convince the judge that my father had written it under duress. When she saw that the judge was leaning in my favor, she paid me a visit. She had Finlay and Gordon hold me while she bragged about how they were going to kill me by throwing me from the window. We were on the fourth floor of the mansion, mind you. Then she would have those two lie under oath that I was so upset over the court fight, I had been contemplating suicide."

"But you got away?"

"Only because a maid knocked on the door. It distracted Finlay and Gordon, and I broke loose and ran." Darlene trembled at the memory. "The first thing I did was take a carriage to the lawyer's, find the will, and flee the city. So long as I'm alive and the will is safe, my sister is thwarted."

"And that story about your father not wanting a woman to run things?"

"Another of my sister's many lies. Mr. Fargo, my father was the kindest, gentlest man you'd ever want to meet. He never believed women were inferior to men."

So there Fargo had it. Two different, conflicting accounts. Which should he believe? Who struck him as being more honest? Charlotte, Finlay, and Gordon? Or Darlene? The question seemed to answer itself. "I think you're telling the truth. I trust you."

"I wish I could say the same." Darlene stood. "You seem like a nice man. But I've been duped before. If you're sincere about helping me, then go back to my sister and tell her you couldn't locate me. I know she's in Yankton, waiting for me to show myself. All I want is to be left in peace."

"You can't hide forever," Fargo said.

"I don't intend to. Only until I can safely sneak back to Philadelphia. Leaving was a mistake. I realize that now. I should have gone to the police, or to the judge, and told them what she tried to do. But I wasn't sure they'd believe me. My sister can be very persuasive."

Fargo rose and hooked his thumbs in his gunbelt. "I'll do

as you want. And if I can be of any more help, let me know."

Darlene seemed like she was about to say something, but she changed her mind. Turning, she hurried toward the house. At the door, she looked back. "Be careful. My sister won't take kindly to being crossed. Never make the mistake of turning your back on her or you'll regret it."

The door swung shut. Fargo walked to the front yard and let himself out the gate. Anger set in, anger at the ordeal Charlotte Weldon had put her sister through, anger at how the Weldons were using him. Somehow he must throw Charlotte off the scent. But how? He reflected long and hard as he made his way to the Grand Hotel. The desk clerk informed him the Weldons were out, and that they had been gone for hours.

Fargo scribbled a note, telling Charlotte he would return around sunset. Then he headed for his own hotel. He was inserting the key to his room when a muted sound alerted him that someone was in his room. Pushing the door inward with his foot, he skipped to the right, the Colt filling his hand.

Seated in the chair was the woman uppermost on his mind. Charlotte Weldon had her legs crossed, her parasol across her thighs, her hat on her knees. Grinning, she said, "Come right in. Make yourself at home."

No one else was there. Fargo closed the door and bolted it so they wouldn't be interrupted. "You're a bundle of surprises."

"Am I, indeed?" Charlotte's mouth curled upward. "Before you ask, I'll tell you. I paid the clerk to let me in. A lot of money, I might add. I thought I could get by with telling him I was your sister, but for some reason he wouldn't believe me."

"One sister too many," Fargo mused.

Charlotte deposited her hat and parasol on the floor. "I'm waiting with bated breath. How did your search go? Have you found my treacherous sibling yet?"

"This soon?" Fargo laughed. "Even in a town the size of Yankton it will take a while. I'll need a week, maybe more."

"You don't say?" Charlotte brushed at her scarlet bangs. "I'd hoped to wrap this up much sooner. I want to be back in Philadelphia by the end of the summer."

"I'm doing the best I can."

Standing, Charlotte said, "Fascinating, isn't it, how quickly our lives change from day to day? Two days ago you and I were total strangers. Now we're the best of friends."

Fargo wouldn't go that far. She came toward him, her eyelids hooded, her supple breasts twin peaks in her dress. "Why are you here?"

"Isn't it obvious? I find you appealing, in a crude, unrefined sort of fashion. I daydream of you and me together. Would you like to make that dream a reality?"

"The two of us?" Fargo could count the number of times he had said no to a woman on one hand. As enticing as the redhead was, she would probably be another rejection.

"Something wrong? Most men drool at the prospect." Charlotte extended her arms, resting them on his shoulders. Her lips were inviting raspberries, her body his for the caressing. "What are you waiting for?"

Fargo was in the midst of an inner war, his conscience against his desire. His manhood twitched, and he raised his hands to embrace her. But at the last moment he stood stock-still.

"No?" Charlotte stepped back. "You're the first man to ever resist my wiles. I must not be as alluring as I flatter myself being."

"You're a beautiful woman," Fargo said, swallowing the lump of raw lust that had formed in his throat.

"Just not beautiful enough? I can't say I'm not disappointed but I'll live with being rejected." Pouting, Charlotte moved to the door. "I'm leaving while I still have a shred of dignity intact." She pointed at her hat and parasol. "Would you be a dear and hand them to me?"

As Fargo complied he heard her throw the bolt. He was bending over when he sensed a rush of movement. Arms encircled his legs, his waist, and his chest and he was smashed to the floor. His elbow smacked a board, rendering it numb. Pinned on his side, he fought to rise but the combined weight of the three men who had jumped him was too much. Sweaty, swarthy faces leered in triumph. They were river rats, viscous ruffians stamped in the same cruel mold as Gar Myers.

"Turn him around," Charlotte instructed them.

Fargo was roughly rotated so he could see the doorway. On either side of it, grinning wickedly, were Finlay and Gordon.

Charlotte claimed the hat and parasol herself, then stood over him. "The great Trailsman. What a joke! You're a dull sluggard, like most men." She poked his cheek with the top of her parasol. "You must take me for a dunce. I've had you shadowed since we met. Not just by my pitiful excuse for brothers, but by these three gentlemen. They took turns so you wouldn't catch on."

The rivermen rubbed salt on Fargo's humiliation by laughing harshly.

Again Charlotte poked at him, spearing the metal tip at his eye. He jerked his head back and it missed, but not by much. "What did Darlene do? Bat those lovely cow's eyes of hers and you melted in her arms?"

An awful dread seized Fargo.

"I knew the minute you found her. I heard about the nice, long talk the two of you shared. So I set up this little reception in appreciation." Charlotte's features were contorted in a mask of raw hatred. "What did she tell you? What did you discuss?" she demanded.

"We talked about how big a bitch you are." Fargo kept an eye on her parasol. He never saw her foot, but he felt it when her shoe rammed into his mouth and blood spurted.

64

Once again Charlotte underwent a drastic transformation. Bestowing a kindly smile on him, she donned her silk hat. "Never mind. I don't need to know what my darling sister said. By this time tomorrow she'll have joined you, and all my problems will have been solved." She snapped her fingers at Gordon. "Get his revolver and the money we gave him."

Chortling, Gordon was all too glad to do it. He removed everything from Fargo's pockets and shoved it into his own.

"Bring it in," Charlotte ordered.

Finlay and Gordon hastened out and returned carrying a large steamer trunk. Closing the door, they slid the trunk over and opened the lid.

"Have you any idea what this is for?" Charlotte asked. When Fargo didn't reply, she held out her right hand to Gordon, who placed a large metal lock in her palm. "It's one of my own. I bought it in St. Louis, the best on the market. It can hold up to three hundred pounds, so it should have no problem holding you."

Gordon gleefully rubbed his hands together. "I can hardly wait. I only wish we could see his face when we dump him in."

"Into the Missouri River," Charlotte clarified. "Out in the middle, where it's deepest."

"Ever tried breathing water?" Gordon taunted.

Charlotte opened her parasol and twirled it. "Let's get this over with. I can't wait to pay my darling sister a visit and tell her what's in store for her."

6

Skye Fargo had a severe cramp in his left leg but it was the least of his worries. He was on his knees, doubled over in total darkness, locked inside the steamer trunk. His arms were behind his back, his wrists bound together. He had also been gagged, thanks to Gordon, by having his own bandanna shoved deep into his mouth. For the better part of fifteen minutes he had been jostled and scraped as the trunk was borne toward the Missouri River by the three river rats in Charlotte Weldon's employ.

Charlotte, Finlay, and Gordon were in the lead, chatting up a storm. Fargo couldn't hear everything they said but he did catch snatches of their conversation. From what he gathered, they were taking back streets and alleys to play it safe. Not that anyone would have second thoughts about a party bound for the levee. But Charlotte wasn't one to take needless risks, and she was worried Fargo might act up by banging his feet against the trunk and making other noises to draw attention to them.

Fargo's hat was gone. The river rats had bumped it off when they dumped him in the trunk. His Colt had been left lying on the floor.

In their haste to bind him and leave, the Weldons had blundered. No one had thought to search him thoroughly. One of the rivermen had gone through his pockets, but no one had checked in his boots. The Arkansas toothpick was still nestled safely in its ankle sheath.

It was Fargo's only hope. Unless he could free himself,

and quickly, he would be dumped in the river and drowned. But try as he might, he couldn't reach the sheath. He couldn't slide his arms low enough to slip his fingers into his boot.

"How much further?" Charlotte Weldon asked.

"Another couple of minutes, ma'am," one of the river rats answered.

Two minutes! Fargo renewed his efforts, struggling mightily, both against the rope and against the trunk's walls. But the cutthroat who tied him had done a good job. The loops were so tight they cut into his flesh. It would take an hour to reach the point where he could move his wrists, even a little, and he didn't have an hour. He *had* to get the toothpick out!

Abruptly, the carriage rounded a corner. The movement caused Fargo to sway as he smacked against the trunk's side.

One of his captors grunted. "Heavy bastard, ain't he?"

"Strong, too," remarked another. "I swear, he almost broke loose when we were tying him."

"Doesn't matter how strong he is," said the third. "Unless he's half fish, he'll soon be dead and we'll each be two hundred dollars to the better."

"I can't wait until this is done with," the first man said. "I'm going to drink grog until it comes out my ears."

The second riverman lowered his voice so the Weldons wouldn't hear. "Doesn't it bother either of you, the idea of helping kill a woman next?"

"For two hundred dollars," the third one said, "I'd murder my own mother."

"I'd do it for fifty," was the first riverman's response.

All three laughed cruelly.

It was Fargo's turn to grunt as they took another sharp turn and he was thrown against the other side. His right knee slipped. Pain wracked his shoulder. But it worked in his favor, for he wound up tilted lower, with his hands much closer to his boots. Extending his fingers, he felt the top of his right boot. Eagerly, he attempted to shove his hand in, but he couldn't quite reach.

Fargo strained his muscles like never before. His shoulders were throbbing with pain and his wrists were in agony but he refused to give up. A fraction of an inch at a time, his fingers crept steadily lower. His index finger brushed the inside of the boot, then his ring finger. The hilt of the toothpick was so close!

Contorting his body to its limit, Fargo smiled when his fingertips touched the knife. He was breathing loudly through his nose, sounding like a winded horse, but he didn't care if anyone heard. Another inch or two would do it! The torment was beyond belief but he wasn't about to quit.

Elation coursed through Fargo when his two fingers finally wrapped the toothpick. But it was short-lived. He still had to pull the knife out with fingers already stretched as far as they would go. Tightening them, he began to slowly ease the knife upward, trying desperately to keep it from snagging on his boot or his pant leg.

The sheath had been designed so the knife was extremely snug and wouldn't fall out while Fargo was riding or running. It now worked against him. Fargo couldn't quite loosen it enough, although he tugged and tugged with every fiber of his being.

Beads of sweat formed on his forehead. His joints and sinews were in misery. But Fargo gritted his teeth against the pain and continued trying. Suddenly the Arkansas toothpick popped loose and he nearly lost his hold. His hands were as sweaty as his brow. Pausing, he inhaled deeply a few times to steady himself, then he carefully reversed his grip and positioned his hands so he could saw at the loops binding his wrists.

It was too late. The clomp of boots on wood told Fargo they'd arrived at the levee's wharf. The rivermen lowered the trunk, jostling him.

"We should hurry, ma'am," one said. "A watchman could

come along at any moment, and he might wonder what we're doing."

"They don't let people roam around down here at night," explained the man who would gladly slay his own mother for fifty dollars. "Not with all the cargo lying about."

"This will only take a second," Charlotte Weldon replied.

Fargo heard her rap lightly on the trunk's lid.

"Still awake in there? You must be rather uncomfortable. But your discomfort will end shortly." Charlotte snickered. "This is what you get for turning against me. For thinking you were so clever. I gather you liked my sister. Was it those soft blue eyes of hers? All that blond hair? In your last seconds I want you to think of her. Think of how you led me to her, and how thanks to you, she will soon share your fate."

Gordon chuckled. "You can be so vicious. I just love it!"

"No one betrays me and lives," Charlotte declared coldly. "No one."

Fargo was sawing at the rope the whole time. The toothpick was razor sharp but it was slow going thanks to the angle at which he had to hold the knife. He heard rustling and then a thunk as something was dropped on top of the trunk.

"Use that," Charlotte said.

The first riverman laughed. "You don't miss a trick, do you, lady?" There was metallic scraping at the top, where the hasp was located. "You even brought your own chain and lock."

"Not that we need them," commented the third riverman. "When I tie someone up, they stay tied. That fella can't possibly get loose."

"Maybe so," Charlotte said. "But if you want to succeed in this world, gentlemen, always cover all contingencies. Planning for the unforeseen ensures success."

"Whatever you say, lady," the first river rat said. "But all that matters to us is our money."

"As soon as we've dispatched my darling sister, the three of you will get what you deserve."

"You're really going to kill your own flesh and blood?" The first man cackled. "Ma'am, if you don't mind my saying so, you're a woman after my own heart."

"Regrettably, I can't say the same. Now do as you were instructed and chain the trunk up and row the damn trunk out on the river."

Fargo was sawing furiously, his whole body damp, every muscle screaming in protest. He almost lost his grip when the trunk was lifted. It swayed as the rivermen locked the chains around it, then carried it to the end of the wharf.

"Someone has to steady the rowboat while it's lowered down," said the third man.

Finlay sniffed. "Don't look at us. We hired you to do the menial labor."

Fargo listened to the sound of someone clambering down from the wharf into the rowboat. But before they could place the trunk in it, Gordon hissed a warning.

"Look! A lantern! Someone is coming this way!"

"It's a watchman!" the first riverman said. "If he spots us, we'll have a heap of explaining to do."

"What do we do?" the third riverman asked, sounding scared.

"We stay calm," Charlotte snapped. "He's still a hundred yards off." She paused. "How deep is it right here?"

"The water?" the first riverman responded.

"No, the empty space between your ears. Of course I meant the water, you pathetic clod!"

The third riverman answered her. "About twenty feet deep at this time of year, ma'am. A little further up, where the boats are tied, the channel is even deeper."

"This will have to do. The watchman will spot us if we move closer to the steamboats. Lower the trunk over the side and give it a shove." Charlotte indulged in some unladylike swearing. "But I don't like it. I don't like it one bit."

"What difference does it make whether the river is twenty feet deep or forty?" Finlay inquired. "The frontiersman will drown, regardless."

"I wish we could haul him back up later," Gordon said. "I've never seen a drowned body before."

Charlotte exhaled loudly. "Morons. I am surrounded by morons." She swore some more. "What are the rest of you waiting for? An engraved invitation? Drop the damn trunk in, and be quick about it."

Fargo braced himself so he wouldn't lose his grip on the Arkansas toothpick. It was well he did. The trunk dipped at a steep angle and he slid against the front, mashing his face and hurting his already split lip. He tasted the salty tang of his own blood anew.

"Hurry!" Charlotte Weldon urged.

Fargo was jostled from side to side. There was a thud, then a loud splash and a hissing noise. His every nerve tingled as he realized the trunk was in the Missouri River. The rivermen had let go and it was slowly sinking toward the bottom. The sensation was sickening. He fought off a wave of panic and renewed his assault on the rope. The temperature rapidly plummeted and he grew quite frigid.

Along with the hissing arose a gurgling noise. Fargo's mouth became completely dry. The trunk was still at a sharp angle so he propped a shoulder against it to gain room to move. A trickling sound added to his woes. Water was slowly seeping in.

Some steamer trunks were more watertight than others. Expensive trunks were lacquered on the outside and insulated on the inside in order to protect their contents should they accidentally be dropped in the drink. Cheaper trunks, those that could be purchased for a few dollars, were little more than thin slats of wood and were next to worthless.

Charlotte Weldon didn't know it, but out of habit she had inadvertently bought Fargo a few precious minutes of life. She was accustomed to buying only the best. So her steamer trunk was the finest on the market. It was temporarily staving off the river's waters. But any second, the mighty Missouri might burst in, and that would be that.

Fargo's wrists were dripping with blood. He wriggled them fiercely, the rope scraping deeper, seeking to work them loose. His fingers were stiff and burned madly. The Arkansas toothpick felt as if it weighed a ton. He sawed and sawed, holding his breath, growing colder and colder, afraid the trunk would start rolling.

A corner sprung a leak and water gushed in. A thin geyser sprayed against Fargo's cheek and neck. Instinctively, he recoiled, bumping his head on the top. The knife slipped from between his fingers and he clutched at it, catching hold of the hilt. As he struggled to firm his grip, the opposite corner began spewing water.

Fargo was weakening. His muscles had been exerted to their absolute limit, and beyond. His arms protested when he pressed the blade against the rope again. Bunching his shoulders, he sheared wildly. Cutting it was next to impossible. Everything was slippery; his hands, the knife, and the rope. He slashed and sliced, connecting with his hands and wrists as often as he did the rope.

Moments later Fargo was thrown backward as the steamer trunk crashed to the river's bottom. He had hoped the impact would be lessened by the thick layer of mud but it was as if he'd fallen off a twenty-foot cliff. Behind Fargo a rending crack sounded. The trunk was starting to break apart. Water poured in around his feet, rising swiftly to his knees, to his chest.

Fargo sucked in the last of the air. In a minute it would be over. His string of luck had finally played out. Just then, the Arkansas toothpick parted the last strand. The rope slid off his wrists. He thrust outward with both his arm and his legs, using the last of his strength. The trunk shattered apart, leaving only soggy planks and loose coils of chain. The next moment he was tumbling in muck. Muddy water sheathed him like a glove. He couldn't tell up from down, right from left.

Fargo's feet came to rest on what must have been the river's bottom. As Fargo spat the gag out of his mouth he sought a glimmer of light, anything that would confirm the surface was overhead. His lungs were being tortured. They wouldn't hold out much longer. Taking a gamble, he pumped furiously, rising much too slowly. Air began to escape from his nose, from his mouth. He simply couldn't hold his breath any longer.

Fargo's senses were reeling. His consciousness blinked in and out. He clawed higher, his arms becoming more and more sluggish. The river was like thick porridge, and there seemed to be no end to it. In a flurry of bubbles, the last of his breath escaped and he couldn't help sucking in water. He felt it entering his nose and mouth. His eyes closed and his arms stopped flailing.

For a few heartbeats, Fargo had felt no sensation whatsoever. Then he was suddenly electrified by an intake of fresh air. A breeze fanned his face. He blinked, and saw steamboats lined up along the bank an arrow's flight distant. Much nearer was a small wharf, the same one the trunk had been dropped from. Tied to it was a rowboat.

Fargo was floating two dozen feet from the shoreline. He saw no one on the wharf, nor any sign of a watchman. Willing his exhausted legs to kick, he slowly swam to shore and wearily climbed onto dry land. Once he was safe, he collapsed. He needed rest, and plenty of it. But he couldn't afford to, not with the life of Darlene Weldon at stake.

Three times Fargo attempted to stand. Three times his legs refused. Finally he succeeded and weaved inland, shuffling like a drunken sot. Angrily, he ripped the gag from where it had settled around his neck. He was dripping water with every stride. His hair and beard were plastered to his head, and every muscle in his body felt raw.

Fury flared. It fueled him, like wood in a boiler engine, lending Fargo strength. He tapped into a reservoir of stamina he didn't know he possessed, becoming stronger the farther he traveled, so by the time he reached a main street he was upright and moving purposefully, his expression enough to scare pedestrians from his path.

Fargo wasn't a bloodthirsty man. He never killed unless he had no other choice. But he was in a killing mood now. He couldn't wait to confront Charlotte, Finlay, and Gordon. He couldn't wait to see *their* expressions when they saw he was alive.

The plump desk clerk was on duty at the Imperial, dusting furniture. "My word!" he exclaimed in horror. "What happened, sir?"

Fargo barreled past without a word. He took the stairs three at a bound and was halfway down the hallway to his room when he saw his door was ajar. A shadow passed across the opening as voices fell on his ears. As silent as a ghost, he moved to the jamb. Not until then was he aware that he still gripped the Arkansas toothpick firmly in his hand.

The voices were familiar. They belonged to the river rats who threw him in the Missouri.

"I don't see why we had to do this, Clements," complained one mercenary. Rearing from the shadows, Fargo saw he was tall and had a hooked nose. "That bitch should have sent one of those hifalutin relatives of hers."

"They're too high and mighty, Frank," said the other, a weasel in human garb. "The kind who like to dish out orders but never take them."

"A pox on all rich bastards," Frank declared.

Fargo peeked further inside, seeing that they were piling his personal effects on the bed; his saddlebags, his spare buckskins, the Henry, the Colt.

"A waste of our time is what this is," Frank grumbled on. "That fella is dead by now. What good does getting rid of his stuff do?"

"She doesn't want anything of his left lying around," Clements said. "He has to disappear without a trace, was how she put it. Let's get it over with. Then we'll go collect our pay and spend the rest of the night in the company of a couple of lovely wenches."

Fargo eased the door inward. The hinges were well oiled. Both rivermen were oblivious to his presence until he spoke. "Think again."

Frank and Clements spun. Shock at seeing him alive rooted them in place for the two seconds it took Fargo to cross the floor in a bull rush. Frank was nearest to him, and his hand swooped to a long knife in a sheath on his left hip. As Frank drew it, he pivoted and lunged to bury it in Fargo's ribs. But Fargo was faster. The riverman didn't see the Arkansas toothpick, held low against Fargo's leg, until it flashed forward and imbedded itself in his chest just under the sternum. Dead on his feet, his heart pierced, Frank oozed to the floor, taking the toothpick with him.

The weasel, Clements, didn't waste time going for his own knife. He sprang to the bed and grabbed the Colt. Gripping it with both hands, he awkwardly thumbed back the hammer as he turned to shoot.

Fargo bounded and slammed into him, driving them both onto the bed, on top of his personal effects. The weasel attempted to press the barrel against Fargo's torso but Fargo grasped Clements' arms, holding the revolver at bay. They fought for control, rolling back and forth.

Clements was an eel. Fargo tried but couldn't pin him. Then they rolled off the bed and crashed onto the floor. Fargo was on the bottom, but it wasn't much of a fall—Clements didn't weigh enough to knock the wind out of him. Snapping his right leg up, Fargo whipped it down again, lancing the spur on the back of his boot into the river rat's leg.

Clements howled and pulled away, seeking to flee. Fargo, holding on to the Colt with one hand, drove his other fist into the man's jaw. It rocked Clements, permitting Fargo to tear the pistol from his grasp. Instantly, Fargo pistol-whipped him, smashing the barrel against Clements' head four times. The river rat slumped onto the floor.

Stiff and sore, Fargo rose. He closed the door and returned to the bed. As much as he would like to change buckskins, he didn't have the time. Instead, he opened his saddlebags, took out a box of ammunition, and replaced the cartridges in his gunbelt with fresh ones. In light of what was to come, a misfire could prove fatal. Jamming his hat on his head, he retrieved the Henry and was about to depart when he bumped against Clements.

What to do with the rivermen?

Opening the window, Fargo dragged the dead man over, verified no one was in the vicinity, and tossed the body out. Next it was Clements' turn. He groaned as Fargo laid hold of him, and his eyelids fluttered open.

"What—?"

Remembering how they had taunted him about being able to breathe water, Fargo remarked, "Hope you can fly." He started to drag Clements toward the window. The weasel squeaked and resisted.

"No! You can't! I was only doing what I was paid to do."

"Let that be your epitaph." Fargo shoved the weasel across the sill, and pushed. The crunch of bone as Clements hit, headfirst, was clear as a school bell, even from three stories up.

Closing the window, Fargo blew out the lamp and hastened down the stairs. The clerk called out his name as he went out the door. Fargo debated running to the stable for his stallion, but by the time he got there and threw on a blanket and saddle he could be almost to the Plumber place. So he ran to the north, the stiff breeze chilling him to the bone.

Right away Fargo noticed something peculiar. The Plumber house was as dark as a tomb. Not a single light shone from any of the windows. Yet it wasn't late enough for everyone to be in bed.

The same dread that had seized Fargo in the hotel room earlier seized him again. He was tempted to barge in the front door but common sense dictated he work around to the rear. The back gate hung wide open, proof others had been there before him. He levered a round into the Henry's chamber as he dashed to the back steps. To avoid stepping on the creaking board, he jumped onto the small porch.

Within, the house was all quiet. Fargo slowly opened the door and slipped inside. No sounds broke the stillness.

The kitchen was to Fargo's left. Near the table lay a crumpled form. At first glance Fargo thought it was Amanda Plumber, but when he turned the body over he saw it was a middle-aged woman he had never met before. One of the boarders, he reckoned.

Climbing the stairs to the second floor, Fargo went from room to room. In one he found the body of a woman of twenty or so lying in a pool of blood, her throat slit from ear to ear. She had been in her nightgown, about to retire, when she was slain.

Fargo hurried back downstairs and crept along a narrow hall to a sitting room. On an end table was a large lamp, beside it some matches. Fargo struck one and applied it to the wick, bathing the room in a golden glow that belied the scarlet stains and splattered drops. Two figures were prone on the carpet.

Amanda Plumber was on her back, her dress drenched in red. Over twenty small puncture wounds dotted her body and limbs. She had been stabbed so many times, she was leaking like a sieve.

Fargo sank onto a knee and pressed his hand against her neck, feeling for a pulse. To his amazement, she opened her eyes.

"I'll go for a sawbones," Fargo proposed.

"Too late," Amanda croaked. "I'm done for and I know it. That short one. He did it. A regular devil, he is." She coughed, dark drops dribbling from the corners of her mouth. "Should've heard him cackle."

"What about Darlene? Did they take her?"

Amanda tried to shake her head but she was too weak.

Swallowing hard, she said, "No. She'd left before—" Amanda stopped, grimacing in agony.

"Before they came?" Fargo was awash with relief.

"Yes. The sweet dear thought it was too dangerous for us, her being here. So she decided to hide elsewhere."

Fargo disliked having to question her, as weak as Amanda was. But he had to find out. "Hide where?" He imagined it would be another boarding house.

"North of Yankton—about ten miles. Our cousin, Hiram, took her." Amanda was growing paler by the second.

North of town was nothing but untamed wilderness. Fargo said as much. "Why take her there?"

"An old cabin . . . on the James River." Amanda clutched at his arm and stiffened. "Oh! Mercy sakes! I hurt so much! Lord, help me!"

They were her last words. She expired with a sigh and a shudder. Fargo closed her eyes, then checked on her brother.

Horace had twice as many wounds, one through his left eye, several through his groin. Yet, incredibly, he, too, was still alive. A spark remained, enough for him to wheeze, "Sorry, mister. I tried. They made me tell. They made—" His hands closed on Fargo's arm. "Watch the canes! The canes!" Always by his sister's side in life, Horace joined her in death.

Fargo's throat was constricted, his temples hammering, as he grimly stood and surged out the front door. Charlotte, Finlay, and Gordon didn't know it yet, but there would be hell to pay before he was done. The Trailsman had a score to settle.

7

It had been a long night.

Skye Fargo's first stop was the hotel where the Weldons were staying. Since he had counted on them leaving at dawn, he was surprised to learn they'd already turned in their room keys and had left. The stableman, a crotchety old cuss, confirmed that "a lovely redhead, two fancy-pants with stupid-lookin' high hats, and four hard cases" had rented horses and rode out less than half an hour before Fargo showed up.

Fargo hurried to his own room, gathered up his belongings, and paid the plump clerk on his way out the door.

"Sorry to see you leaving, sir," the younger man said. "I won't forget about looking up that lady you mentioned. I just hope she likes me."

More likely, Fargo mused, Sally would take pity on him. Before she was through, she'd show him there was more to life than living with his mother. As Fargo made for the entrance, the clerk snapped his fingers.

"Say! I almost forgot! The marshal wanted to talk to you."

"What about?" As if Fargo couldn't guess.

"A while ago, a couple of bodies were found right outside. One fellow had been stabbed and the other had a busted neck. The marshal needs to see everyone registered here. But half of them are out for the night, so he said he'd stop by in the morning."

"Thanks for letting me know." Fargo shouldered the door

open and was gone. Sticking around to answer a slew of questions wasn't in the cards. He had to reach Darlene Weldon before her sister did.

The James River was a tributary of the Missouri. It crossed the Dakota Territory from north to south, joining the Missouri east of Yankton. But since the James meandered widely, a rider could travel due north from Yankton and strike it before too long.

No trails existed to point the way. Other than occasional cavalry patrols, few dared venture into the wilds. It was Sioux country, and the Sioux were growing to resent white encroachment. Bloody clashes had occurred with growing frequency. Hunters and trappers had been found bristling with arrows, many often scalped.

Fargo couldn't understand what had gotten into Amanda and Horace. They shouldn't have let Darlene go. Maybe Darlene had convinced them it was her only hope. Maybe she thought it was the only way to elude Charlotte, and had made up her mind to do it no matter what. Perhaps the Plumbers had sent their cousin along to protect her.

It was all conjecture. Fargo would learn the truth only when he caught up. He rode until well past midnight and saw no trace of anyone. It was possible that instead of heading overland, Charlotte's bunch had gone east to the James River, and from there would follow it north. Which would take them even longer.

Confident he could spare the time, and to keep the Ovaro rested, Fargo made a cold camp and spread out his blankets. The yipping of coyotes lulled him into a dreamless sleep, and the chirping of birds woke him to a pink tinge painting the eastern sky. He saddled up and trotted off.

The new day broke crisp and clear. Deer grazed in the hollows and along the fringes of woodland. When Fargo reached the James River he turned to the north, paralleling it. He hadn't gone more than a few dozen yards when he noticed fresh tracks. Two shod horses and a mule. They had passed that way sometime the previous evening. No other prints were evident. Fargo felt confident Charlotte and her killers were still far behind.

It felt great to be in the wilderness again. Fargo watched a red hawk pinwheel high in the sky. He saw elk across the river, and a small herd of buffalo further off. The region was a paradise. How long it would stay so remained to be seen, what with more homesteaders flocking in every year.

By Fargo's reckoning he was about a mile from the cabin when he made a troubling discovery. Not more than an hour ago, a lone horseman had emerged from a belt of cottonwoods and examined the tracks left by Darlene and Hiram. The rider's mount wasn't shod, and where the man had climbed down to inspect the ground were moccasin prints. Then the rider had sped to the northeast, crossing the river.

A Sioux scout, Fargo suspected, who had gone to inform others. Whether there would be trouble depended on whether he belonged to a hunting party—or a war party. Tapping his spurs against the Ovaro, Fargo presently came to a series of low hills. On an impulse he climbed to the crest of one to scan his back trail. Far to the south, strung out in a line, were seven riders.

Fargo cantered down the hill, Sioux to the northeast, Charlotte at his back. Returning safely to Yankton would take some doing. Loosening the Henry in its saddle scabbard, he moved briskly on until he rounded a bend and beheld a clearing ahead. In the center stood a dilapidated structure that once had been a cabin, but now consisted of random logs supporting a roof that had long since collapsed. A bay, a sorrel, and the mule were picketed nearby. They watched him closely, the bay nickering as he halted in front of the ruins.

From a stand of trees smoke curled. The fragrant aroma of coffee was in the air. Both would draw hostiles like honey drew bears. Shaking his head in disgust, Fargo yanked out the Henry and walked toward the stand, only to stop cold when the muzzle of a rifle poked past the buckled corner of the cabin and someone nervously commanded him to halt.

"That'll be far enough, stranger. We don't want no company. Turn around and hightail it. Pronto."

"Hiram Plumber?" Fargo said.

A small, droopy-eyed man in his thirties stepped into the open, gripping a Sharps. Homespun clothes covered his wiry frame. "Who in tarnation might you be? I don't recollect us ever meeting."

Fargo scoured the hills beyond the trees. As yet, the Sioux hadn't appeared. "Amanda told me where to find you. You've got to head back to Yankton right away."

"Now why would we want to do that when we just got here?" Hiram responded. "For all I know, this is a trick of some sort. What proof do you have my cousin sent you?"

"Where's Darlene Weldon? She knows me."

Hiram jerked his head. "Up the river a piece. Said she needed to wash off the trail dust in a pool yonder."

"You let her go off alone?" Fargo started toward the James but the click of the Sharps hammer dissuaded him.

"Stay right where you are, mister. The lady doesn't want to be disturbed." Hiram sidled to the left. "We'll wait until she's done. Then you'd best pray she does know you, like you claimed. Because if you're one of those polecats out to hurt her, you'll answer to hot lead."

"We don't have time to waste," Fargo said. "For her sake, take me there. I'll even give you my guns if that will make you feel safer."

His appeal fell on deaf ears. Hiram went on covering him with the rifle. "In case you ain't caught the drift yet, the lady is taking a bath. She needs her privacy. So we're staying put." Pleased with himself, Hiram grinned. "This is the old Meeker place. Hardly anyone remembers it but me. He was the first white fella to plant roots in these parts. Made his living trapping and whatnot until the Blackfeet paid him a visit."

"How did Darlene hear of this place?"

"Horace and me have hunted up this-a-way a few times. So when Amanda mentioned how Darlene needed to lay low a spell, Horace suggested it. No one would think of looking for her here."

"Unless they found out about it," Fargo said. He hated being the bearer of awful tidings. But it couldn't be helped, and might goad Hiram into taking him to Darlene. He stepped toward the man. "Brace yourself. Amanda and Horace are dead. The ones who are after Darlene are to blame, and they're hard on your trail."

Disbelief twisted Hiram's features. "Dead? They can't be. No one can get the better of Horace. He's as strong as an ox."

"Even an ox can be brought down by a pack of wolves. I'm sorry," Fargo said sincerely.

Hiram trembled as if about to have a fit. "You're lying!" he practically shouted. "You're making it up to rattle me! You must be one of the scum after Miss Weldon." He thrust the big Sharps at Fargo and curled his finger around the trigger. "Make your peace with your Maker. You're about to die."

Fargo hadn't counted on this. He couldn't bring himself to shoot the man, yet neither could he stand there and let Hiram put a hole in him the size of his fist from close range. "Think. If I was one of them, would I ride right up to you? No! I'd pick you off from ambush."

"Who knows?" Hiram retorted, pausing. "Maybe you're trickier than most. You figured that you could get me to let down my guard, to turn my back. Well, it didn't work!"

Fargo's mind raced. As agitated as Hiram was, he might squeeze the trigger at any second. Rushing him wouldn't do, not with the Sharps primed to fire. So Fargo resorted to one of the oldest ruses around. He gazed over Hiram's shoulder and said, "Don't kill him yet, boys. Just take his rifle."

It worked. Hiram spun. Fargo arced the Henry's stock up and around, dealing Hiram a solid blow to the skull. Soundlessly, his legs weakening like soggy paper, Hiram collapsed. Fargo stripped him of the Henry and a Green River knife, hid both behind a fallen beam just inside the cabin, and jogged upriver.

Bent blades of grass guided Fargo around two bends to a pristine setting, a stretch of lowland where the gurgling river was bordered by lush forest on both sides. High grass sprung up along the bank and flowers grew in abundance. Sparrows, robins, and jays sang merrily. A rabbit was nipping at a stem, totally unafraid. But none of it held Fargo's interest. His gaze was riveted on the exquisite creature cavorting in a wide pool.

Darlene Weldon's naked skin glistened. She swam in circles, shot to the surface, and dived again, displaying superbly formed limbs and marvelous satiny thighs. Her golden hair was molded to her shoulders and upper back. High on her chest were two taut peaks, her breasts as near to perfect as nature ever wrought. As Fargo looked on, she bent at the waist, dipped her head under the water, and arched her tawny legs upward. He glimpsed the blond triangle at their junction, and when she parted her legs wide, he glimpsed even more.

His manhood surged. Holding the Henry in front of him to hide his excitement, Fargo walked to the edge of the bank, then turned to be polite. Glancing over his shoulder for a last tantalizing glimpse of her wondrous form, he called out, "Miss Weldon! You've got to get out, right now!"

Fargo thought she would screech or frantically try to cover herself, but she showed no shame at being seen. Rather, she swam slowly toward him, a mysterious smile curving her luscious mouth, her breasts exposed with every stroke.

"To what do I owe this great surprise, Mr. Fargo?"

"You're in great danger. Your sister is on her way here with a bunch of hired killers."

Darlene's smile evaporated. "How can that be? No one knows where I am except the Plumbers."

Fargo would have preferred to break the news to her gently, but the circumstances being what they were, he gave it to her straight out. "Amanda and her brother are gone, Darlene. Your sister had them murdered. It was Horace who broke down and told her where to find you."

"No!" Darlene's face went rigid with shock. She stopped swimming. "Dear Lord! Please tell me it isn't true! Not kindly Amanda and sweet Horace!"

"Charlotte is about an hour behind me," Fargo mentioned. "So if we hurry, we can be long gone by the time they arrive." He shared the rest of his tidings. "That's not all. A party of Sioux is on to you, and there's no telling when they might show."

Darlene couldn't get over the terrible fate of her friends. "The Plumbers were decent people, Fargo. They'd never harm a soul without cause." Tears began to flow. "They were only trying to help me."

"You need to get out and get dressed," Fargo coaxed. But she was too distraught. Quietly weeping, she kept saying over and over, "Why them, God? Why them?"

Fargo beckoned. "Please, Darlene. If we don't light a shuck, your sister will get her hands on you. Is that what you want?"

Darlene started to wade out, blinking to clear her eyes. "This is the last straw! Amanda and Horace won't have died in vain! I'm tired of running. Let Charlotte come. This is where I make my stand."

"You're not thinking straight," Fargo said, striving his utmost not to be distracted by her naked charms. But what man wouldn't be? He devoured the sight of her lips, two ripe cherries, and her breasts, so full and round.

"You're wrong. I'm thinking straight for the first time in a long while." Darlene moved toward her clothes, which she had draped over a high bush. Her firm backside was a delight, her thighs as creamy as milk. "We'll wait for Charlotte. Then she and I will have it out. One way or another, my ordeal ends today. No more innocents will lose their lives because of me."

Fine sentiments, Fargo reflected, but her anger and despair were blinding her to the peril she was in. "There are seven of them and only three of us."

"I don't care how many helpers she has. It's strictly between her and me." Darlene snatched her undergarments. "Now, if you would be a gentleman and turn your back, I can pretend to have a modicum of modesty."

Reluctantly, Fargo did as she bid. But it was hard to tear his eyes off her voluptuous figure. She had the kind of body great artists like to portray on canvas, that great sculptors liked to immortalize in marble. The sound of rustling told him she was swiftly dressing.

"Where's Hiram?"

"He thought I was working for your sister. I had to knock him out." Fargo peeked back and saw she already had her chemise and long cotton drawers on. Facing forward, he sighed.

"More pain and suffering," Darlene said bitterly. "But you're not to blame—my sister is. She taints everything she touches, ruins everyone she meets. She's caused untold misery over the years, and it's high time she was stopped. Once and for all."

"I agree," Fargo said, "but we should pick a better time, a better place." Especially with the threat of a Sioux war party hanging over their heads.

"You and Hiram can leave if you want. I'm not going anywhere."

Fargo held his peace while she finished dressing. When she appeared at his elbow, he gripped her arm and hastened toward the cabin. "We'll douse your campfire and saddle your horses. In fifteen minutes we'll be gone."

Darlene dug in her heels, resisting him. "Weren't you listening to a word I just said? I intend to confront Charlotte, come what may."

"And what do you think Finlay and Gordon and those men your sister hired will be doing while you and she are settling things? Twiddling their thumbs?" Fargo shook his head and resumed pulling. "She'll have them tie you up and throw you in the river, like they did to me. Or maybe she'll torture you, like she did the Plumbers."

"They threw you in the river?"

"Into the Missouri." Fargo didn't go into detail. The memory was too vivid, too harrowing.

"My sister is a fiend," Darlene said, sorrow-struck. "An inhuman monster! How could she turn out like she has? How can the two of us be so different when we were raised in the same house, by the same loving man?"

Fargo had no answer for that one.

"I've denied the truth for too long," Darlene told him. "After what she did to the Plumbers, I suspect her string of victims is a lot longer than I have ever conceived. That maybe she killed for the first time when she was only ten."

"How's that?" Fargo asked. He was keeping his eyes on the country to the east for sign of the Sioux. While he had once spent some time among them, it had been years ago. Many might not remember him. Then, too, the Sioux weren't one big tribe. There were many branches, or sub-tribes, like the Oglalas, the Brules, the Sans Arcs, the Minniconjous, and the Hunkpapas. Some were more hostile toward whites than others.

Darlene was relating her tale. "When we were children, I had a close friend by the name of Claudia. She and I went everywhere together. Charlotte despised her, even though Claudia was always nice to Charlotte." Darlene's voice grew strained. "One day, Claudia and I went to the lake to play. I forgot a doll and ran back to the mansion to get it. When I returned to the lake, Claudia had disappeared. I looked and looked but couldn't find her. I told the butler, who sent for my father." She slowed. "The searchers found her body in some reeds. Everyone assumed she'd gone into the lake and accidentally drowned. Now, I can't help but wonder."

Fargo didn't have any doubts. Charlotte had surely killed Claudia. How many more had she disposed of over the years?

"My father's death might not have been from natural causes, either," Darlene said. "About two years ago he took sick. He had terrible stomach cramps all the time, so our doctor prescribed a special diet. I always thought it strange that Charlotte volunteered to do the cooking for him from then on. But I justified it by thinking she was making amends for all her bad behavior in the past."

"Let me guess—your father got worse and worse."

"He wasted away, yes. The night he died, we were at his bedside. He was holding both our hands, and I couldn't stop crying. When he passed on, I turned around, and Charlotte was actually smiling. An evil smile, if ever there was one." Darlene closed her eyes, then opened them again. "That was my first inkling of the nightmare in store. A week later, when the will was read by my father's lawyer and Charlotte found out everything had been left to me, her hatred knew no bounds."

They were almost at the last bend before the clearing. Fargo let go of her and shifted the Henry from his left hand to his right.

"Going to the judge or the law won't stop her, will it, Fargo?"

"Not without proof," Fargo said.

Darlene clutched him, bringing them both to a stop. "Be honest with me. What would you do if you were in my shoes?"

"It's not for me to say." Fargo wasn't being evasive. Some decisions were too important, too personal, for other people to make. "But keep one thing in mind—your sister won't rest until you're dead."

"Maybe, just maybe, I can reason with her."

Fargo felt sorry for Darlene. Her ideals were blinding her

to the truth. She was like a horse with blinders on, stranded on the brink of a cliff. "And maybe, just maybe, you can talk a charging grizzly out of ripping you to shreds."

"You're saying there's no hope? Either I kill her or she'll kill me?"

Suddenly, out of the high grass, rushed Hiram Plumber. Waving a thick limb, he bellowed, "Damnation! Get away from that no-account, Miss Weldon! I'll protect you!"

Darlene stepped between them. "No, Hiram! Don't! He's a friend. We can trust him. Put that down."

"He is?" Hiram looked severely disappointed that he couldn't bash Fargo's head in. "But he hit me. Clouted my noggin'."

"You were about to shoot me," Fargo reminded him.

Darlene kept going. "Pack up, Hiram. My sister is on her way. We must be gone before she arrives."

Fargo overtook her. "What changed your mind?"

"You did." Darlene smiled. "It's about time I grew up. I refuse to play the fool any longer. If it's come down to either her or me, I don't want it to be me. My death would serve no purpose other than to reward her for all her scheming."

"You've made the right choice," Fargo said, patting her back. Darlene didn't flinch like she had at the Plumbers'. Her smile widened and she touched his hand, her fingers warm against his.

"I'm in your debt, Fargo."

"Please, call me Skye."

Movement to the south drew Fargo's gaze to the top of a hill. Riders had appeared. Charlotte's bunch were making better time than he expected, or else she had sent several scouts on ahead. "We don't have any time to spare."

Darlene looked in the same direction. "How long before they get here?"

"Three-quarters of an hour. Less, if they push hard."

Hiram was right behind them, muttering to himself. He tapped Fargo on the shoulder. "Where the dickens did you put my Sharps and my knife, mister? I hunted all over and couldn't find them."

"In the cabin."

"Dang. I didn't poke my head in there because I was afraid the roof would fall on me. All it would take is a hard sneeze."

Tendrils of smoke still wafted skyward from the trees. The fire had burned low, though, so all it took was a few handfuls of dirt for Fargo to extinguish it. He helped Hiram saddle the sorrel and the bay, then walked to the riverbank while Hiram saw to tying packs on the mule.

Darlene was staring into the water, her countenance as downcast as a rainy day. "I'm partly to blame, you know," she said without glancing up.

"For what?"

"Claudia's death. My father's. The murders of Amanda and Horace. And who knows how many more." Darlene brushed a hand across her brow. "If I'd stood up to Charlotte sooner, if I hadn't deceived myself into thinking she's better than she is, all of them might well still be alive."

Fargo didn't hold back. "That's bull. If you had caused problems for her sooner, she'd have killed you long ago. You wouldn't have been around to help your father, or to save the Plumbers." He squeezed her wrist. "What's done is done. We can't change the past."

"Hey!" Hiram yelled. "What's the holdup? I thought you two were in an all-fired hurry to get the hell out of here?"

Fargo assumed the lead. With Sioux to the east and Charlotte's cutthroats to the south, that left north and west. He chose the latter. His aim was to swing in a wide loop that would bring them back to the James River behind Charlotte's outfit. From there, they could proceed to town without incident.

Hiram handled the mule, the lead rope wrapped around his saddle horn. He brought up the rear, chomping on a wad of chewing tobacco. When they had gone a quarter of a mile he hollered, "Mister! Take a gander! Are they who I think they are?"

Silhouetted on the crest of a hill to the east were four horsemen. Even at that distance, Fargo could tell two of them wore little or no clothing, and that one was armed with a bow and arrows. "Sioux."

"Only four? Hellfire, I can lick that many with one arm tied behind my back."

Fargo remembered an old mountain man who was fond of saying that fools and their lives were soon parted. The arrival of the warriors, though, was timely. With any luck, the Sioux would see to it that Charlotte Weldon's bloody spree came to an end. It couldn't have worked out better if he'd planned it that way.

More than likely, the Indians had spotted them. But on the off chance the warriors hadn't, Fargo reined toward a rocky gulch that offered cover. He trotted into it, Darlene close on the Ovaro's hooves. He didn't give much thought to all the flat rocks littering the sides until a sinuous shape sunning itself reared up as he went by. "Look out!" he shouted.

It was a big rattler, and the snake began to shake its tail as Darlene's sorrel drew near. The horse shied, nearly throwing Darlene off. She lost her grip on the reins and had to lunge to reclaim them. By then it was too late.

The rattler struck.

8

To Darlene's credit, she hauled on the sorrel's reins and tried to veer aside, but the rattlesnake was just too close. Its fangs sank into her mount's foreleg. Nickering in fright, the sorrel reared again. Darlene clung to the saddle but she couldn't hold on, and tumbling, she landed on her side. The sorrel reared a third time, its hooves smashing to earth within inches of Darlene's head.

Skye Fargo had wheeled the Ovaro to help. Slapping his legs against the pinto, he brought it alongside the sorrel and snatched at its bridle. The snake was already slithering off under the rocks. To avoid it, the sorrel bounded to one side, out of Fargo's reach. Another moment later it was racing up the right-hand slope, its mane and tail flying.

"I'll catch him!" Hiram cried. Releasing the lead rope, he trotted in pursuit.

Fargo vaulted from his saddle and helped Darlene to stand. She was shaking, her hands and face smudged, her left palm gashed. "No bones broken?" Fargo asked, exploring her arms.

"No. I don't think so."

Fargo steered her toward a waist-high boulder. "Have a seat. A close shave like that would spook anyone."

Darlene's knees gave out. She would have pitched forward had Fargo not caught her. She leaned against him, her cheek on his neck, breathing heavily. To calm her, he stroked her luxurious hair.

"Sorry," Darlene said. "Nothing like that has ever happened to me before. My heart is beating madly."

Fargo could feel it, hammering against his chest. The warmth she gave off, and the softness of her hair, combined to give him thoughts better suited for another time and place. His skin commenced to prickle as if from a heat rash.

"How can I possibly stand up to my sister when a little fall has me so upset?" Darlene asked.

"You could have been killed," Fargo said, but she wasn't listening.

"I've never been particularly brave, I'm afraid. When problems reared up, I'd always ignore them until they went away, rather than meet them head-on." Darlene mustered a lopsided grin. "Poets are notorious for running from reality."

It was her frayed nerves talking. Fargo said as much and hugged her. She responded by embracing him and lightly pecking him on the throat. Her face rose, and for several seconds they were nose to nose, mouth to mouth. He had an almost overwhelming desire to smother her with burning kisses, to slide his tongue deep into her mouth, but he resisted it.

"Thank you for coming to my rescue," Darlene said huskily.

"My pleasure."

"Perhaps we should check on Hiram. He might need our help."

They rode double. Fargo swung her up behind him, seized the mule's rope, and clattered up out of gully. The warriors on the hill were gone, and there was not any evidence of Charlotte's men, either. Hiram was still riding hell-bent for leather after the sorrel, which was fleeing toward a small plain.

Fargo held the Ovaro to an easy lope. The feel of Darlene's breasts on his back and her arms around his waist did little to quench the fire she had unwittingly stoked. He was glad when she sat up a little straighter.

"Tell me, kind sir. Do you always make a habit out of rescuing young maidens in dire distress?"

"Sometimes it seems that way."

Darlene rested her chin on his left shoulder blade. " 'Ancient of days! August Athena! Where, where are thy men of might? Thy grand in soul?' "

Puzzled, Fargo swiveled and she grinned.

"From *Childe Harold's Pilgrimage* by Lord Byron. He was one of my favorites when I was growing up. Romanticist, dreamer, champion of liberty. Byron was my idol, my knight in poetic armor. Have you read any of his works?" Darlene asked in all seriousness.

"No."

"None?" Darlene was astonished. "Surely you've heard of him, though? How about this snippet from 'She Walks in Beauty'?" Darlene thought a moment. " 'She walks in beauty, like the night of cloudless climes and starry skies. And all that's best of dark and bright meet in her aspect and in her eyes.' "

"Can't say I've heard it," Fargo admitted, thinking that Byron could well have written it about her.

"Mercy me. What do people out here do for entertainment? How do they spice up their lives?"

"We get by as best we can," Fargo said. "Most are too busy making ends meet to bother with much else."

"How sad," Darlene declared. "Poetry is a way to escape this drab existence and reach for the stars. I couldn't live without it."

The sorrel had stopped fleeing. Head drooping, sides heaving, it was whinnying repeatedly. Hiram had reined up and forked a leg across his saddle for better balance as he raised the Sharps to his shoulder.

"What's he doing?" Darlene asked in alarm.

Hiram glanced around as Fargo brought the Ovaro to a halt. The sorrel was foaming at the mouth and its legs were wobbling. "Stinking snake," he growled. "This animal wasn't mine. I rented it. Now I'll have to make good."

Darlene slid off. "You can't mean to shoot it! Maybe the bite won't prove fatal. We should wait and see."

Squealing, the sorrel fell onto its front legs. Drool cascaded over its lower jaw and it nickered pitiably.

"Rotten rattler," Hiram ranted. "I'd like to stomp it to a pulp and make soup out of it." He sighted down the Sharps.

"Don't shoot," Fargo said.

"No?"

Fargo dismounted and walked over to the stricken animal. The blast would carry for a mile or more. It might bring Charlotte, or the Sioux—or both—on the run. Bending, he drew the Arkansas toothpick. "We should do it quietly."

"For God's sake, don't!" Darlene flew at Fargo and gripped his arm. "Let the poor creature be! It might recover!"

As if to show how wrong she was, the sorrel keeled over onto its side. Its legs kicking feebly, it tried to rise, fighting the inevitable to the last.

"No!" Darlene mewed. Clasping a palm to her forehead, she reeled. "This awful, brutal world! Is there no end to its savagery?"

Fargo pried her fingers loose, hunkered by the horse, and pressed the tip of the toothpick's blade to the animal's throat. Its eyes were rolling in their sockets and its breathing had grown shallow. As he tensed to plunge the steel in, the sorrel convulsed and was still. Grateful, he replaced the knife.

"Lousy snake," Hiram carped again.

Fargo stripped off the saddlebags. They contained a hairbrush, a comb, and some of Darlene's other belongings. He transferred them to his own saddlebags, then stepped into the stirrups and offered her his hand. With a last look at the sorrel, she accepted.

"Such a senseless death."

"Show me one that isn't," Fargo countered. A sweep of the horizon disclosed no one was after them—yet. Cutting the stallion to the south, he traveled for over an hour without mishap. Broken country rolled before them.

"Can we rest soon?" Darlene asked. "I have a cramp in my leg. I'm not accustomed to so much riding."

Fargo gave the horses a breather in a shaded hollow rimmed by brush. Hiram, still grumbling about the loss of the sorrel, climbed to the top to keep a lookout. Fargo sat with his back propped against a gnarled tree and idly plucked at blades of grass.

Darlene unfastened the top three buttons of her dress. "Growing hot, isn't it?"

"It will grow a lot hotter," Fargo said.

"How do you stand it?"

Fargo shrugged. "You get used to it after a while."

"No, I don't mean the weather. I mean life out here in general. Indians, badmen, snakes and fierce beasts. Doesn't it make you want to dig a hole and crawl in?"

"We can't run from life," Fargo said.

"That's been my whole problem. When I was young I hid in my poetry. When father died and Charlotte showed her true colors, I ran off and fled west." The breeze picked up, fanning Darlene's hair, framing her face in a golden halo. "Being brave doesn't come easily. It's a lot harder to dredge up courage than succumb to cowardice."

"You're doing fine."

Darlene smiled. "You're being kind. But the truth is, I don't cope well in a crisis. Look at how I behaved when that rattlesnake bit my horse."

"If it had bit mine, I'd have been more upset than you were," Fargo said, seeking to bolster her spirits.

"You're just saying that."

But Fargo wasn't. His wanderings had taken him from one end of the country to the other, and rarely had the Ovaro let him down. It was as dependable a mount as any a man could ask for.

"Do you ever wish for something different? Ever wanted to give up the wide open spaces and live back East?"

"I'd rather be shot," Fargo quipped. The mountains and the plains were as much his home as the Weldon mansion had been hers. "I like being free. I like being able to do as I want, when I want."

"And back East we can't?"

A yell from the rim interrupted them. Hiram was frantically beckoning.

"Stay with the horses," Fargo instructed Darlene. Snatching the Henry, he climbed, crouching as he neared the top so he wouldn't be visible from afar. Hiram was on his knees, pointing in the direction they had come.

"Someone is tracking us."

Sure enough, a pair of horsemen were on their trail, approximately half a mile out. Fargo squinted against the glare, confirming that one of the pair was naked from the waist up. "Indians."

"How can you tell?" Hiram said. "To me, they ain't more than a couple of stick figures. Do you reckon the Sioux are after our scalps? Or maybe just curious?"

"I won't know until I talk to them." Fargo began to descend. "When they're close enough to pick off with that cannon of yours, come tell me."

Hiram made a sound that resembled a chicken being strangled. "Not so fast. You're fixing to jaw with them? What good will that do?"

"We'll find out what they want. Maybe avoid spilling blood."

"But they're just Injuns. Why not plug them and be done with it?"

Fargo's estimation of Plumber fell a notch. Hiram shared the same outlook many settlers did, namely, the misguided belief that the only good Indian was a dead one. "Indians are just like us. Some are good, some aren't. Let's find out which these are before we make worm food of them."

"Whatever you say. But it seems to me you're going to a lot of bother for nothing."

Fargo jogged down to their animals and wrapped the

reins and the lead rope around handy scrub. Sometimes the scent of Indians caused mounts to spook. Many warriors used special concoctions consisting of bear fat and other pungent ingredients to stiffen their hair or slick their bodies.

"What are you doing?" Darlene strolled over. "Can I help?"

"You can be the bait." Fargo scanned the hollow for the best place in which to hide.

"I beg your pardon?"

Fargo patted a level spot a few yards from the horses. "I want you to sit here with your back to the north rim. In about five minutes, a couple of curious Sioux are going to show up, and I want them to get a good look at you."

Shock took Darlene back a step. "Are you serious? I've heard all sorts of horror stories about the atrocities Indians commit. What if they try to abduct me? Or simply shoot me down where I sit?"

"I won't let them take you," Fargo vowed. "And warriors don't generally kill white women outright. Not when the women can be put to better use."

Darlene put a hand to her throat. "Oh! I'm taking an awful risk, then, aren't I?"

"If you don't want to do it, just say so," Fargo said. But he knew anything she did to distract the two warriors would help greatly. "I'll be right there." He indicated an erosion-washed trough just above them on the opposite slope.

"You'll protect me?"

Fargo could hardly blame her for being nervous. "With my life," he said, and meant it.

Darlene went to the mule, opened a pack, rummaged inside, and pulled out a large book which she cradled in her elbow as she took a seat. "The sonnets of William Shakespeare. They always soothe me when I'm troubled. Perhaps they'll keep me calm enough to go through with this without fainting." She grinned.

Hiram Plumber came hopping down the slope like an

oversized frog. "They'll be here directly," he announced. "What's the plan?"

Fargo gave him a push toward a cluster of bushes off to the right. "Lay low over there. Don't shoot unless I do."

"Whatever you want. I just hope to hell you know what you're doing." Muttering, Hiram sprinted for cover and dropped flat.

The trough Fargo had selected for himself was two feet deep and about twenty feet in length. He lay on his left side, the Henry in front of him, and removed his hat. From his vantage point, he could see the rim better than the other two, so he was the first to see the warriors. The Indians had dismounted and were now leading their horses. In the forefront was a stocky warrior wearing only a breechclout and moccasins. His companion had on a faded army shirt, torn brown pants, and a broad-brimmed brown hat.

They weren't Sioux, Fargo realized. The one in the breechclout looked to be part Bannock and part white. The other seemed to be Pawnee, but his features betrayed mixed lineage as well. White men branded their kind half-breeds, and generally shunned them.

Suddenly Fargo recollected his talk with the old-timer in the Lucky Dollar. His stomach churned as he remembered the old man speak of Moon Killer's band of cutthroats. He'd made a terrible mistake, an error in judgment that could cost Darlene Weldon dearly. He watched as the two breeds grounded their reins and crept toward the rim. They were skilled stalkers. Flattening, they snaked to the edge and peered over. Their surprise at finding a woman was apparent. They scoured the hollow, then slid back and whispered to one another. Fargo gathered there was a disagreement. The one in the breechclout wanted to leave, probably to inform their band. But the one in the army shirt, the Pawnee, had a different idea, and he eventually won out.

Both men cautiously rose. Holding their rifles with the barrels down, they strolled into the hollow as if they were on a Sunday jaunt. Darlene had her back to them and was busy flipping pages. They spread out to approach her from either side, their dark eyes constantly roving this way and that. They weren't greenhorns, these two.

Darlene's head snapped up. She'd heard them. She glanced toward the trough as if seeking some clue as to what she should do, but Fargo didn't show himself yet.

The Bannock and the Pawnee halted. "What you doing, woman?" the Pawnee demanded in heavily accented English.

Casually closing her book, Darlene twisted and smiled. "Why, hello there. I'm reading. Wherever did you two come from?"

Gesturing, the Pawnee answered, "We hunting near river. We see riders long off." He openly ravished her with his eyes. "You not alone."

Fargo shot to his feet, the Henry at his waist, his hat in hand. "No, she's not," he said good-naturedly. The pair froze. "We're on our way back to Yankton." Donning his hat, he walked to the left, at an angle away from Darlene, so when the shooting broke out she wouldn't take a stray slug.

"Only you?" the Pawnee said. "We think maybe there be two white-eyes."

"Just me," Fargo lied. "Where are you two from? Is there a village near here?"

"We be Oglalas," the Pawnee said, gesturing vaguely to the south. "Come long way. Hunt elk."

"Last I heard, there are plenty of elk in Oglala country," Fargo commented. He should know, having lived among them for a while. Reaching the bottom of the hollow, Fargo pivoted on his heels so he was sideways to the breeds, presenting them with a smaller target.

"You say my tongue forked?" the Pawnee asked belligerently.

"Don't get your dander up," Fargo responded. "You're as honest as I am, for all I know. A man can hunt wherever he wants."

The Pawnee grunted. "My name Cunning Fox." He was pretending to be friendly but he had all the warmth of high-country snow.

"Who's your friend?" Fargo played along.

"Him Otter Tail. Him not speak much white talk." Cunning Fox couldn't keep his eyes off Darlene's hair. Since most Indian women had dark hair, blondes were held in high esteem. He was smitten below the belt, as it were.

"Sit awhile," Fargo invited them. "We don't mind the company."

Cunning Fox translated for the benefit of Otter Tail. Both squatted, their rifles across their thighs, Otter Tail fingering the breech of his.

"Seen anyone else hereabouts?" Fargo asked.

"Other white-eyes," Cunning Fox said. He held up the fingers and thumb on his right hand, curled them to his palm, then held up two more fingers. "One be a white woman. Hair like fire."

Fargo fished for more information. "We know them. Fact is, we're supposed to meet them but we lost our way. Where are they now?"

"Last see near river," Cunning Fox said, not taking his gaze off Darlene. "Near old wood lodge."

"Are they still alive?" Fargo hoped to the contrary.

Cunning Fox wasn't listening very well. "Alive?" he repeated. As the significance hit him, his hawkish features pinched tight. "What else they be?"

"Maybe staked out and skinned alive," Fargo said. "Or tied upside down to a tree, with fires lit under them. Moon Killer is always coming up with new ideas."

At the mention of the renegade's name, both Cunning Fox and Otter Tail imitated statues. "Who be Moon Killer?" the former asked slyly.

"Some say he's part Blood, part Crow. Others say he's part Ute, part white. You must know. How long have you been riding with him?"

"We?" Cunning Fox said, and he did not appear so cunning now. Licking his lips, he slowly placed both hands on his rifle.

"Moon Killer has a band of twenty to thirty men," Fargo said. "All half-breeds like him. They were seen in this area a week or so ago."

"We no ride with Moon Killer," Cunning Fox declared. "We Oglalas. Sioux. Hunting elk."

"And I'm the Queen of England." Fargo's humor was lost on them. He had thumbed back the Henry's hammer when he was in the trough. Now he slowly hiked the barrel, bringing it level.

Cunning Fox whispered to his companion, and in unison they began to stand. "You think maybe you so clever, white-eye? Maybe you not."

The two renegades swept their rifles up but Fargo beat them, the Henry booming like thunder in the restricted confines of the hollow. Cunning Fox was smashed off his feet onto his back. Otter Tail almost had his rifle high enough when Hiram Plumber's Sharps thundered. The slug cored Otter Tail's head from ear to ear, taking a sizeable chunk of Otter Tail's brain with it.

Fargo ran to Cunning Fox and slammed his foot down onto the other's rifle as the renegade strained to lift it. Collapsing, Cunning Fox glared.

"Where's Moon Killer and the rest of his men?" Fargo wanted to know.

The Pawnee tried to spit on him but missed.

"Tell me, or I'll leave you here for the coyotes and the buzzards," Fargo said. Among some tribes it was held that those mutilated in this world would bear the wounds and scars in the next. The secret fear of their warriors was to die missing limbs, or worse.

"I never say." Cunning Fox defied him. From a gaping hole in his chest came a sucking sound.

"How many are with him?" Fargo persisted.

Cunning Fox bared his teeth. "Plenty enough to kill you. Plenty enough to steal woman and horses." Clenching his hands, he resisted crying out as his body was wracked by anguish.

Hiram arrived, reloading the Sharps. "Want me to finish the vermin off?"

"Save your ammunition," Fargo replied. They would need every cartridge they had it they ran up against Moon Killer and his band.

"White dogs," Cunning Fox rasped. It was his last comment of any kind. The wound gushed red, and so did his nose and lips.

Fargo turned to see how Darlene was holding up. Wide-eyed, she was staring aghast at the brains, bone, and gore that had ruptured from Otter Tail's head, splattering the grass. Her book had fallen to the ground, forgotten. "Don't look," he said, moving in front of her to spare her the horrid vision.

"I've never seen anyone shot before," Darlene said quietly, and swooned.

Dropping onto his knees, Fargo lifted her head to his lap and stroked her golden hair. She had done well, proving she had more courage than she gave herself credit for. "Drag the bodies off, will you?" he directed Hiram.

"Why me?" was Plumber's rejoinder. "I swear, you're bossier than Amanda ever was, and that takes some doing." Indulging in his favorite pastime—muttering—he nonetheless did as he was requested.

Darlene wasn't unconscious long. Stirring, she opened her eyes and moved to sit up. "What's your rush?" Fargo said, his hands on her slender shoulders. "Rest a minute."

She glanced at the dead men, then averted her face. "I'm sorry. I told you I'm no use in a crisis."

"Quit apologizing. The next time you won't be so squeamish."

"I pray to heaven there *is* no next time," Darlene said. Her bosom was heaving and falling rhythmically. "What was that business about Moon Killer? Who is he?"

"The worst butcher north of the Pecos, a breed who hates whites and Indians alike."

"Whatever for?"

"Most whites despise half-breeds. Most Indians don't want anything to do with them." Fargo saw Hiram Plumber let go of Otter Tail and run toward the top of the hollow. "It soured Moon Killer so bad, he can't get the acid out of his system. He just naturally hates everyone who hates him."

Hiram came to an abrupt stop. "Get up here!" he shouted.

"What is it?" Fargo asked. As if he couldn't guess.

"There's more of them a-coming!"

9

There were, as Cunning Fox had said, plenty more. From the rim, Skye Fargo spied a knot of riders approaching from the north *and* a bunch approaching from the east. Moon Killer had heard the shots, Fargo reasoned, and split up his band. Escaping was now doubly difficult. They couldn't head south because the renegades to the east would spot them. Their only hope was to race westward, further into the wilderness, and ever farther from Yankton.

"Do we make a stand?" Hiram inquired eagerly.

"The two of us against two dozen guns?" Fargo snorted. "It would be the Alamo all over again."

"Shucks. I ain't scared."

"You should be." Fargo looked for the horses belonging to Cunning Fox and Otter Tail. They had run off, spooked by the gunfire.

Darlene, with her precious book of sonnets clutched to her bosom, had climbed on the Ovaro. She slid back to give Fargo room as he forked leather, her arms quickly looping around his waist. Fargo hunched low over the saddle and took the slope on the fly. Once on open ground, he let the stallion have its head.

Fargo knew that the cloud of dust they raised would alert those after them. So he wasn't surprised when the riders to the north angled away from the hollow, in hot pursuit. The bunch to the east hadn't noticed yet because of the trees and brush along the hollow's rim, but they would soon enough.

It would take some doing to elude the renegades. Men

like Moon Killer were keen judges of prime horseflesh. They had to be. Fast mounts with exceptional stamina kept them one step ahead of the army and the law, and one step away from the gallows.

Fortunately for Fargo, the Ovaro could hold its own against any horse alive. But the same couldn't be said of Hiram Plumber's bay, and even less so of the mule. They had gone about a mile and a half when the mule showed signs of flagging. Burdened as it was by heavy packs, it wouldn't be long before the chase took its toll on the struggling beast.

Yet they couldn't stop. Not yet. Not until Fargo found a spot where they could hold off the renegades. Deep into the rugged hills they sped, Darlene clinging firmly to him, Hiram muttering a blue streak and tugging on the lead rope to force the mule to keep up.

On a high ridge Fargo drew rein so their animals could catch their wind. A dust cloud in the distance pegged the location of the renegades. Moon Killer's surly wolves had narrowed the gap considerably, but they were still well out of rifle range.

"Will they give up eventually?" Darlene asked.

"Not if they know about you," Fargo answered honestly, and regretted it when he saw how it affected her.

"Are all females west of the Mississippi fair game for every brute not behind bars?" Darlene angrily asked.

"Afraid so."

"How barbaric. At least back in the East men treat women with civility." Darlene ran a hand through her flaxen hair. "The age of romance is long dead, alas. It died with Byron and Keats."

Hiram had been listening. "Speaking of dying, I'm not hankering to join my cousins in the hereafter anytime soon. So if either of you have a notion how we can get out of this mess with our hides intact, my ears are open."

"We keep running," Fargo said.

"You call *that* a great idea?" Hiram muttered a few

choice oaths. "I reckon this is what I get for letting Amanda talk me into helping out. If I had any blamed sense, I'd have stayed home and got drunk."

Darlene's features became tinged by sorrow. "Nobility, thy name is Hiram Plumber."

"Huh?" Hiram said. "What are you babbling about now? I ain't hardly noble, lady. In this godforsaken country, a man can't afford to be."

" 'Few are my years, and yet I feel the world was never designed for me,' " Darlene recited wistfully. "How right Lord Byron was."

Hiram scratched his stubbly chin. "I don't rightly know much about lords and ladies and the like. But I do know, missy, you have some downright addlepated views. You think the Almighty created this world just to please you? What makes you more special than the rest of us?"

"You missed my point," Darlene said, and frowned. "Oh, why bother. It's like trying to teach a dog to quack like a duck."

"See? There you go again." Hiram chortled. "Maybe you're the one who should write a book. Tarnation! I might buy it just to laugh at your silliness."

"Can we move on?" Darlene requested.

They forged westward until well past noon. The dust cloud to the rear neither gained ground nor lost any. All their animals were caked with sweat when Fargo called another halt on a bluff. Sliding off, he examined the mule. It had stumbled several times during the ascent and now stood with its head drooping.

"Give that ornery critter ten minutes and it'll be raring to go," Hiram said.

Fargo knew better. "We're leaving it here."

"Like hell we are, mister. I haven't raised a fuss about you giving the orders, but I draw the line at turning that animal over to Moon Killer."

"Then you would have two animals to pay the stableman for," Darlene said with biting sarcasm.

"For your information, lady, the mule is mine. It's not the cost. I've had her pretty near four years, and I hate to think she'd end up in the bellies of those damnable breeds."

"They would *eat* it?"

Hiram walked to the mule and rubbed its neck. "Don't you eastern folks know anything? Some Injuns, like the Apaches, rate mule meat the best there is. They'd sooner eat a mule than a cow. Moon Killer and his boys aren't that choosy. With over twenty mouths to feed, they'll eat anything they can catch."

Darlene moved toward the edge. "The more I learn, the more I loathe." Dust streaked her dress and face and had dulled the luster of her golden mane. She swatted at an insect, coughed, and gave up in frustration.

Fargo stretched his legs by walking in small circles that brought him up next to her. "Are you all right?"

"Why wouldn't I be? My own sister is out to murder me. A pack of mad dogs is baying at our heels. I'm miles from anywhere under blistering sun, suffering the platitudes of a bumpkin who cares for his mule more than he does for people." Darlene gave another halfhearted slap at the bug with her sleeve. "If my life were any better, I'd be overcome with joy."

"You're still breathing."

"Being alive is cause for celebration?"

"Surviving is. Out here, a person never knows from one day to the next if they'll be around to greet the next dawn."

Darlene absently leaned against him. "Survival of the fittest, is that it? In case you haven't noticed, I'm pitifully weak. I wouldn't last two days out here on my own."

"Was it weak of you to buck your sister? Weak of you to try and protect Amanda and Horace by going off into the hills? Weak of you to act as bait?" Fargo draped his arm across her shoulders and pressed her close. "You're a lot stronger than you think."

Darlene raised her head. "Thank you. I appreciate your kindness. There is a lot more to you than meets the eye."

She smirked. "Although what meets the eye is quite pleasing in its own right."

Hiram began muttering to his mule. "Did you hear that, Jezebel? They're making cow eyes at one another. Now he'll probably ask me to hold off the renegades while they go to pluck daisies."

Fargo turned. "We can't outrun Moon Killer dragging your mule along."

"I'm not leaving her," Hiram declared, "and that's final."

"You'd die over a mule?" Darlene interjected.

"Lady, she's the best friend I've ever had, next to Horace. I'd die for her and be damn proud to do it."

"Could Jezebel find her way home alone?" Fargo asked.

"She might," Hiram said. "She's smarter than I am. But I ain't letting her out of my sight."

Fargo had one last idea. "Is she saddle-broke?"

Hiram pulled out his chaw and bit off a piece before answering. "What's that got to do with anything? We don't have a saddle to spare." His mouth stopped chomping a second. "Oh. I get it. Dump all the packs so one of us can ride her."

"She'll last longer without all that weight," Fargo said.

"True enough. Let's do it. I'll take Jezebel and the lady here can ride my bay."

Darlene smiled at Plumber. "You'd give up your horse for me? That's very considerate of you. I'm touched."

Hiram snickered. "Touched in the head, maybe. I ain't doing it on your account. Jezebel is a contrary gal, like most women. She's particular about who she lets straddle her. Anyone other than me, she bites and bucks and won't take two steps. I just don't want you to get her all agitated."

"You're switching mounts to spare your mule's feelings?" Darlene asked.

"Why are you so blasted surprised? Wouldn't you spare the feelings of somebody you care for?"

"Jezebel is a *mule*."

"So? She's every bit the lady you are." Hiram spat tobacco, wiped his mouth with the back of his sleeve, and set to stripping off the packs.

Darlene grinned at Fargo. "I think I finally understand the difference between life out here and life in the East. In the East we keep our lunatics in asylums. Out here you let them run loose."

Fargo laughed. Hiram started muttering again and tossing the packs every which way. Inspecting them, Fargo found that most contained nothing but clothes. From one he pulled a shimmery gown.

"Let me see those," Hiram said. He reached into the same pack and extracted several more elegant dresses. "I thought you said all this stuff was essential?" he huffed at Darlene.

"It is. Those are the best garments I own," she responded. "Amanda helped me pack them before you arrived."

"Lordy!" Hiram said. "We've been wearing poor Jezebel to a frazzle toting a bunch of clothes all over creation." He cast the dresses down. "And you have the gall to call *me* a lunatic?"

"Some of the things I brought are quite useful," Darlene said defensively. "The pots and pans, the coffeepot, my sewing kit."

Hiram held up another pack. "What do we do with this one? There's nothing in here but books."

"My poetry books!" Darlene said, grabbing the pack from him. "I couldn't live without these. Most I've had since childhood."

"They weigh a ton," Hiram admonished.

Darlene appealed to Fargo. "Please don't make me discard them. They're my treasures. One was a gift from my mother."

As much as Fargo would like to grant her request, he had to side with Plumber. "Put a few of the ones you like the most on the bay. We'll hide the rest in the rocks and come back for them another time."

"If we can," Hiram said.

Darlene was heart-stricken. Kneeling, she sorted through the dozens in the pack, selecting four.

Hiram was going through the other packs. Suddenly he straightened. "Will you take a gander at this? I ain't seen anything this pretty since that filly at the dance hall who had three gold teeth."

Sunlight sparkled on a small folding telescope plated with strips of silver. Fargo took it and trained the lens on a distant crag. It stood out in stark detail. According to what was engraved on the tube, the telescope had a magnification factor of fifteen. "Why didn't you tell us you had this?" he inquired.

Darlene was fondling her book on Keats. "That silly thing? A store clerk in St. Louis sold it to me when I went in to outfit myself for my trek West. I've never used it and had forgotten it was even there."

Moving to the rim, Fargo saw that their pursuers were now under a mile away. He used the telescope, hoping to count how many there were, but the cloud of dust they raised hid them from view. From the size of the dust cloud there didn't seem to be as many as he initially had supposed. Certainly not more than a dozen. "Let's light a shuck," he advised.

They fled westward again, deeper into the heart of the wilderness, the mule holding her own, much to Hiram's delight. Fargo missed having Darlene ride double with him, missed the warmth of her body and the feel of her breasts against his back.

Along about the middle of the afternoon, Fargo called another halt. They had stumbled on a shallow stream. While the horses slaked their thirst and Darlene and Hiram rested, he climbed a tree and resorted to the telescope again. Their pursuers had also stopped, on a far-off hillock, and were drinking from canteens. He could see them clearly now, and they weren't who he thought they would be.

Charlotte Weldon had swapped her dress for a riding outfit. Finlay and Gordon, though, still wore their expensive suits and high hats and were carrying their ever-present canes. Of the four hard cases they had hired, Fargo pegged two as rivermen and two as gunmen. A lanky gun-shark who packed two pistols was talking to Charlotte.

Fargo lowered the telescope. What had happened to Moon Killer? he wondered. Had it been the renegade's band approaching the hollow from the east? If so, where had Moon Killer gotten to? He'd have found the bodies of Cunning Fox and Otter Tail, and given his bloodthirsty nature, Moon Killer wouldn't rest until he had dealt with those responsible.

Raising the telescope again, Fargo scanned the countryside. About a mile south of the hillock, in a gully, dozens of men and horses were resting. Breechclouts and leggings were common, and a few of the men had feathers in their hair. One, bigger than the others, sat next to a tall horse with a primarily grayish coat marked by spots on its rump. The coloration was typical of Appaloosas, a special type of horse bred by the Nez Percé Indians. And according to reports, Moon Killer rode one.

The renegade was shadowing Charlotte Weldon, Fargo deduced, waiting for the right moment to strike.

Fargo worked out the recent sequence of events in his head. It had been one of Moon Killer's scouts, not the Sioux, who had found Darlene and Hiram's trail back by the James River and gone for help. Four more of Moon Killer's men had shown up later and two of them followed when Fargo led Darlene and Hiram west. The other two had waited for the rest of the band. As fate would have it, that was when Charlotte and her boys had appeared on the scene. One of her men must be a fairly competent tracker because they had tracked Fargo and his companions clear to the hollow.

When Moon Killer joined his scouts, he'd headed due west, thinking to catch his quarry that much sooner. He had discovered the bodies of Cunning Fox and Otter Tail, and now he was biding his sweet time, waiting to exact revenge. He would wipe out Charlotte's bunch first, then do likewise to Fargo's little group.

That was how Fargo figured it, at any rate. The only reason Moon Killer hadn't struck already was because Charlotte and her men were well armed and alert. To Fargo's recollection, the wily renegade always preferred stealth to force. He was notorious for catching his enemies when they least expected it, preferring swift, brutal attacks from ambush.

Charlotte Weldon didn't know it yet, Fargo mused, but she was as good as dead. Now Fargo had to ensure the same fate didn't befall the two people he was responsible for. Climbing down, he walked to where Darlene lay on her back, an arm across her eyes to shield them from the sun. Her dress accented her womanly attributes, clinging as it did to her bosom and her long legs.

"See anything?" Hiram asked.

Fargo told them, adding, "Charlotte can't catch us before nightfall, so we're safe enough until morning. With any luck, Moon Killer will attack her before too long. The men she hired won't help much against as many killers as he has."

Hiram clapped his hands. "Hot damn! One of our problems will be solved! Then all we need do is give that breed bastard the slip."

Darlene sat up. "My sister won't stand a prayer, will she, Skye?"

"Seven against twenty or better?" Fargo let the odds speak for themselves. The thing that worried him was whether Moon Killer had sent men ahead to keep an eye on them. A few renegades might be spying on them at that very moment. A sweep of the terrain revealed no one, but the killers might be too savvy to show themselves.

"What will they do to Charlotte?" Darlene asked.

"You don't want to know," Fargo said.

Hiram was less tactful. "What do you care, anyhow, lady? After all she's done to you, you should be glad. She'll be paid back in full for all the suffering she's caused." He chortled. "Those bucks will each take turns. When they're good and tired, they'll start in with their knives and—"

"Enough," Fargo said more gruffly than he intended. Darlene was wringing her hands in distress. "Try not to dwell on it," he suggested.

"How can I not? She's my sister. Granted, she's as evil as they come. But she's still my sister. I can't sit by and let her suffer like that."

Fargo placed a hand on her shoulder. "There's nothing you can do."

"Hell, there's nothing any of us can do, even if we want," Hiram threw in. "Which I sure as blazes don't. I've got my own skin and Jezebel's to think of."

The look in Darlene's eyes troubled Fargo. He thought she had come to terms with herself and accepted what had to be done. So much the better now that Moon Killer was doing it for them. She shouldn't be so disturbed.

"If it was *your* brother or sister, you wouldn't be so eager to see them die," Darlene said to Hiram. "Or what if it was your stupid mule?"

Plumber rose up from the ground, fuming. "Don't you be talking about my Jezebel like that. Lady or not, I won't stand for it. Why, if Moon Killer were to steal her, I'd defy him and his whole pack of mangy badmen to save her. That's how highly I think of my Jezzy!"

Fargo decided to move on. Every half an hour he stopped briefly to use the telescope but the situation never changed. Charlotte stayed on their trail, and Moon Killer continued to stalk her. As the shadows lengthened, he turned his attention to finding a safe site to spend the night. He'd rather push on, but the horses and the mule were too exhausted.

Darlene hardly spoke the remainder of the afternoon. Preoccupied, she plodded along with her head sorrowfully bent.

Hiram stopped muttering, for once. He continually stroked Jezebel, encouraging her to keep up.

A low ridge offered the protection Fargo wanted. It afforded a sweeping vista of the land to the east, and the slope leading up to it was barren of cover except for a few pines. It would be hard for anyone to sneak up on them. More pines at the crest provided shelter from the wind. The only drawback was a lack of water for the animals, but Jezebel and the horses had drank their fill at the stream and were more in need of rest.

Fargo allowed a small fire after piling a ring of rocks high enough to screen it from prying eyes below. Darlene went into the bushes to clean herself up while Fargo took Hiram to gather wood.

Plumber was in a jolly mood. "By this time tomorrow night we should be in the clear. Moon Killer will take care of the ones after us, and while he's busy with them, we can slip off. I figure we'll be in Yankton by the morning after."

"If all goes well," Fargo remarked.

They gathered enough dead limbs to last them the entire night. Fargo agreed to keep watch until midnight, at which point Hiram would take over.

Filling his coffeepot with water from his canteen, Fargo was opening the Arbuckle's when Darlene Weldon emerged from the undergrowth. She had undergone an astounding transformation. Her hair had been brushed to a sheen, the dust wiped from her face and hands, and she had changed garments, putting on a lacy dress more suitable for a formal ball in the big city than the remote wilds of the Dakota Territory.

Even Hiram was impressed. "My goodness!" he blurted. "You're almost pretty enough to make a fella give up being a bachelor."

"Thank you," Darlene said, doing a curtsy. She was smiling contentedly, quite a change from her earlier doldrums.

"Nice to see you happy for a change," Fargo said.

Darlene deposited her saddlebags by her saddle. "I've

come to realize a few things. As you once reminded me, we can't change the past. Only the future. I guess my life was preordained the day I was born. Now I've got to embrace my fate."

Hiram produced his chaw. "That's being sensible, lady. All the squawking in the world won't change a hen into a rooster."

Fargo wasn't entirely sure what that had to do with anything, but it made Darlene laugh. He finished with the coffee and set the pot on to boil. From his saddlebags he took a bundle, unwrapped it, and handed a piece of the contents to Darlene.

"What's this?" She sniffed at it, skeptical. "I've never seen anything quite like it before."

"Pemmican," Fargo said. "Buffalo meat, dried and pounded up. Then fat and berries are added. I get mine from a Shoshone woman I know. It lasts as long as jerky but it's a lot tastier."

"Don't mind if I do," Hiram said, coming over and helping himself. He bit off a chunk, mixing it with the tobacco already in his mouth. "That's strange. I can't hardly taste it."

Darlene nibbled at hers, chewed a bit, and smiled. "It is rather good, isn't it?" She ate in earnest, her hunger overcoming her trepidation. "How much do you have?"

"Enough to last the three of us until we reach town," Fargo said. A musty fragrance wafted on the breeze, perfume scented like vanilla. He caught Darlene watching him from under hooded eyes, and inwardly grinned.

"All that time in the saddle has made me sore," she commented. "I'd like to go for a stroll. Do you think it's safe?"

"Only if one of us goes with you," Fargo said.

Hiram was hunkered by the coffeepot, anxiously waiting for it to brew. "Don't look at me. I ain't letting Jezebel out of my sight. I don't want those damn renegades to make off with her when my back is turned."

Fargo didn't want to act too eager, so he sighed and said, "I guess it's up to me. We won't be long, Hiram."

"Sure you won't. And I fell out of the sky with the last rainstorm."

Darlene slid her arm through Fargo's. "I hope you don't mind."

Fargo couldn't think of anything he would mind less. They entered the pines, her shoulder brushing his, the rustle of her dress enticing in and of itself, her perfume adding spice to the night's air. A stone's throw from their camp they came upon a grassy circle not much wider than a bed. Darlene faced him.

"This will do, don't you think?"

Fargo's lips covered hers.

10

Kissing some women was like kissing a limp rag. They had all the fire and passion of a block of ice. Kissing others, however, was the most joy a man could know, an experience as heady as the strongest ale, as potent as the best whiskey, as addicting as cards. It was, as the old phrase had it, heaven on earth, or the closest mortal man could know.

Skye Fargo never made excuses for his addiction. He hungered for women like some men did for gold or opium. Beautiful women drew him like flames drew a moth. And more often than not, the feeling was mutual.

Darlene Weldon was a prime example. She craved him as much as he craved her. Her kisses were molten honey, her tongue silken ecstasy, her body tingling with warmth and carnal desire. She glued herself to him as if seeking to crawl inside of him, showing the side of a proper lady few men ever saw; the basic, human side, the side that showed the same yearnings all women did. Her tongue delved deep into his mouth, then swirled with his in an electric dance.

As Fargo's hands roved from her shoulders to the small of her back, he shifted his eyes to scan the surrounding woods. He must never forget that some of Moon Killer's men might be out there. He must always be alert.

It was hard to do, though, with Darlene doing her utmost to arouse him to a feverish pitch. Part of him wanted to forget all his cares and troubles, and to totally abandon himself to their lovemaking. But he dared not. In a hotel it would be different. When they reached Yankton, if she proved willing, he would do just that. For now, he must always keep one eye and both ears open.

That didn't mean Fargo couldn't enjoy himself. Far from it. As her tongue probed into his mouth again, he folded his lips around it and sucked as if it were a stick of sugar candy. She groaned softly, deep down at the base of her fluttering throat. Each of her panting breaths was a furnace blast, and growing hotter by the moment.

Fargo slid a hand between their bodies to cup her right breast. Darlene moaned, her hips grinding into him. Through the sheer fabric he felt her nipple harden, becoming a rounded nail that dug into his palm as he gently massaged and squeezed. His other hand stroked her lustrous hair, so soft, so pliant.

"Ohhhhh," Darlene whispered when they broke briefly. "It has been so long. So very, very long."

Fargo didn't pry. It wasn't of any consequence. He kissed her cheeks, her eyebrows, her eyelids. He nibbled on the edge of her ear, then sucked on her lobe. She arched her spine, her nails biting into his biceps.

"Ahhhh. You make me feel so good."

The compliment was mutual. Fargo's manhood was straining against his buckskin pants, eager for release. He pressed it to the junction of her thighs, the heat she radiated warming him to the bone.

Fargo glanced toward their camp. Through the trees, the glow from their small fire was barely visible, as was the hunched-over figure of Hiram Plumber. Plumber's back was to them, and he appeared to be adding a few short limbs to the blaze.

The sudden closing of Darlene's right hand on his rigid member made Fargo forget all about their feisty companion. Her fingers delicately wrapped around him as if his throbbing redwood were a fragile butterfly she was afraid of damaging.

"Goodness," Darlene husked.

A lump formed in Fargo's throat as she stroked him, up

and down. Then her hand slid between his legs to fondle him there. Her brazenness was a delightful surprise. He would have expected her to be too timid, too shy, to be so forward.

One good turn deserved another, folks like to say. So Fargo slid his own hand between her legs and was treated to a gasp, a fluttering sigh, and the sagging of her quivering body against his own. His forefinger pressed hard against her dress and underthings, rubbing the entrance to her womanhood. It elicited another groan, much louder than the first.

"Oh, Skye. You do such wonderful things to me."

She didn't specify what sort of things, but Fargo could guess. He rubbed her a few more times, causing her legs to close around his fingers, her mouth devouring his. While she continued to fondle him, her other hand roamed up his back to his hair.

Fargo started to ease her to the grass, then hesitated. He had half a mind to take her standing up. That way he could keep an eye on the woods. But when she gripped him by the shoulders and anxiously pulled him down on top of her, he didn't resist. He had to stay alert, yes, but his attention demanded more immediate concerns.

Their bodies molded together in a delightful play of opposites; hers pillowy and yielding, his muscular and hard. She began to undo her dress, and Fargo helped, giving her flesh a kiss after each button or hook was undone. When he shifted onto his side so she could have access to the lower buttons, she winced.

"Ouch. That hurts."

Fargo's Colt was gouging into her. Unbuckling his gunbelt, he placed it right beside them, the holster within quick reach. He scanned the trees again but saw nothing out of the ordinary. One by one he parted her garments, revealing her ample breasts in all their glory. And they were truly superb; full, high mounds crowned by twin rosebuds that jutted upward. Their allure was impossible to resist. Fargo enfolded one in his mouth, flicking the taut nipple with his tongue.

"Yessssssss!" Darlene cooed. "Oh, yessss!"

For the longest while Fargo dallied, alternating from one heaving mound to the other, licking and sucking and lathering them until Darlene was trembling with raw abandon. Her legs were opening and closing, her hips rising and lowering, her ripe mouth parted in greedy anticipation.

Fargo's left hand dipped down below her slim waist and slowly hiked her dress up higher. When the hem reached her knees, he plunged his calloused hand underneath, his probing fingers gliding under satiny fabric until they made contact with the bare skin of her inner thigh.

Darlene gripped his shoulders, her eyes widening. "I want you so much."

Fargo could tell. Her thighs were scorching. He moved his hand higher, caressing them, until he came to her venus. Uncovering it, he ran a fingertip from front to back, marveling at how deliciously wet she was. He inserted a finger partway, just enough to tease, to tantalize, and she heaved upward as if seeking to join the stars.

"Ah! Ah! More!"

Darlene's body was quaking. When Fargo slid his finger all the way in, she wrapped her legs around his waist, pulling him closer. Her mouth clamped onto his, her long tongue snaking into his mouth. Fargo pumped his finger out and in, just once, and Darlene nearly lifted him off the ground.

"Again! Don't stop!"

Fargo obliged, using his finger to excite her like never before, plunging it in to the knuckle. Her inner walls rippled with each thrust. Her warm hands found their way up under his shirt and kneaded his abdomen, his chest, his back. Darlene's mouth never left his except for occasional low cries of pleasure. None were likely to be heard by Plumber, and if they were, well, Fargo didn't care.

Darlene's nails sank into Fargo's lower back. He stiffened, then inserted a second finger. She bucked up into him in regular rhythms, setting a tempo he matched with the rhythm of his strokes. In and out, in and out. Without her being aware, Fargo rose slightly, high enough to lower his pants down around his knees. And high enough to align his manhood with her opening.

In a smooth motion, Fargo pulled his fingers out and rammed his pole in. Taken by surprise, Darlene threw back her head and opened her mouth wide as if to scream, but no sound emitted. Then she clamped herself to him, her hips matching each of his thrusts.

They climbed toward the pinnacle, Fargo rocking on his knees, Darlene a volcano on the brink of erupting. Her release triggered his. When she thrashed and clawed and flung herself at him, gushing like a spring river, he could no longer hold back. He crested, the night seeming to burst with fireworks more spectacular than those in Yankton.

Darlene bit him to stifle her shriek of release, her teeth sinking into his shoulder deep enough to draw a trickle of blood. Her movements gradually lessened. Darlene's legs levered less and less, until at length she subsided and lay quiet except for the rising and falling of her chest and little mewling sounds she made with each breath.

Fargo rolled onto his back, his hand automatically seeking the Colt. A northwesterly breeze was rustling the trees and in the distance coyotes were in full chorus. Other than that, no sounds disturbed the tranquillity of the night. He let himself relax, closing his eyes and savoring the momentary peace.

Darlene eased onto her side, facing him, and rested her cheek on his chest. Her hand found his hair and she twined her fingers in it. "Thank you."

"Any time."

Giggling, Darlene kissed his scruffy chin. "It's unfortunate we come from such different worlds. I would love to make you a permanent part of mine."

Fargo didn't respond.

"As it is, I know I'm dreaming, indulging in more wishful thinking. Just as I've been doing my whole life. My fate was set in stone long before I was born."

"Oh?" Fargo recalled her saying something similar earlier.

"There's no use fighting the inevitable. I've tried, and look at where it's brought me. I'm on the run from my own sister."

"What else could you have done? Let her murder you?" Fargo couldn't quite understand what she was getting at.

"All I'm saying is that there comes a time when a person has to accept their lot in life and do what has to be done regardless of their personal feelings. All these years I've been hiding from the truth. From myself. It's time I owned up to who I am and the responsibility I have to the Weldon name."

Fargo assumed she was referring to being the proper heir to the Weldon fortune. "You'll do fine. Your father would be proud."

Darlene twisted her neck to gaze heavenward. "Wherever he is, I hope he can see me. And I hope he's looking down and nodding in approval." She placed her mouth on Fargo's and rimmed his lips with the tip of her tongue. "I will never forget what you've done, the lesson you've taught me. You, and that idiot, Hiram."

"What did he teach you?" Fargo asked. "Other than never eat food and chew tobacco at the same time?"

Chuckling, Darlene answered, "His affection for his mule opened my eyes to how wrong I've been. He would die for Jezebel."

Fargo would do the same for the Ovaro and mentioned as much.

"See? Both of you have something you're willing to die for. Can I do less?" Darlene lowered her cheek and idly sketched invisible circles on his broad chest with a fingernail. "My father always said that Weldons must never shirk

123

their duty. I have a duty to him and to the family, and I won't fail."

For a while they lay undisturbed, Fargo smoothing her hair, Darlene lost in thought. The hoot of an owl roused Fargo into sitting up, and he suggested they get dressed.

"Was that a real owl?" Darlene asked. "I was told that Indians are remarkably adept at imitating wild animals."

"It was the real article," Fargo assured her. "We're safe." And were there renegades skulking about, the owl wouldn't have made its presence known. Hiking up his pants, he strapped on his revolver and pulled his hat brim low.

Sitting up, Darlene began to dress. She turned her back to him, shy now that she wasn't in the grip of lust. When they rose, she clasped his hand. As they strolled back to the fire, she hummed to herself.

Hiram was sharpening his knife on a whet stone. Smirking, he said, "I about figured you two wouldn't show until daylight. Thought maybe you'd gotten lost."

Fargo poured coffee for himself and Darlene. She gulped it down, then asked for another cup, which she drank almost as fast.

From then until Hiram turned in, they made small talk. Darlene related how kind and loving her father had been, how he had taken Charlotte and her on scores of family outings to parks and the shore when they were small. Charlotte always hated the outings, but Darlene loved those special times together when they were as close to being a real family as they ever came to being.

"I never had much of one," Hiram remarked. "My pa kicked me out the door when I was ten. Told me I was done slacking. That it was high time I made my own way in the world."

"How did you live?" Darlene asked.

Hiram spat tobacco. "However I could. Sweeping floors, as a clerk, repairing shoes—you name it. Then my cousins, Amanda and Horace, got a notion to travel west. It would be a new start for us, Amanda said. After she took it into her head to settle in Yankton, Horace and me hired on to load and unload steamboats down at the levee." Hiram paused. "You should have seen him tote bales and crates. No one could lift more than Horace. He could do the work of three men."

Fargo believed it.

"I miss him," Hiram said. "Maybe he wasn't the smartest fella alive, but he was kin. And kin is always special."

Darlene was staring into the fire, a strange expression on her face.

"Well, enough jawing for one night," Hiram said. "It's about time I got some sleep. Fargo will be waking me up to take my turn before I know it."

Darlene surprised Fargo by staying up late, downing cup after cup of coffee. She said that she couldn't sleep close to the fire because the light would keep her awake, and she moved her saddle closer to the horses and spread out her blankets. "Thanks again, handsome," she said before retiring.

Not long before nudging Hiram awake, Fargo walked to the rim. Neither Charlotte Weldon nor the renegades had made the mistake of making camp where their fire could be seen.

Hiram was snoring loud enough to be mistaken for a buzz saw. He was slow to stir to life. Sputtering, and still half asleep, he swatted at Fargo's hand, muttering, "I paid my five dollars, sweetie. I can sleep as long as I want."

Fargo poked Plumber in the ribs with the toe of his boot. Blinking sleepily and scratching under an arm, Hiram sat up.

"Damn. Why did it have to be now? I was having a dream about a dove in a frilly red outfit that would give a man fits."

"Keep your eyes skinned," Fargo said as he sank onto his own blankets. "Wake me before sunrise if I'm not already up."

"Will do, big man," Hiram said, yawning. "Don't fret.

You're as safe with me on guard as you were in your mother's womb."

The long hours spent on the run had taken their toll. As accustomed as Fargo was to traveling long distances, he was so tired that within seconds of lowering his head onto his saddle, he was asleep. Ordinarily he was a light sleeper. The slightest noise would awaken him. So maybe it was having made love to Darlene that accounted for why he slept more soundly than was his habit and didn't awaken until the warbling of a bird snapped him fully awake.

Fargo was annoyed to see the crown of the sun perched on the eastern horizon. The sound of snoring turned him toward the fire, which had burned itself out. Hiram was lying beside the ring of rocks.

Worried that Charlotte or the renegades might be sneaking up on them, Fargo bounded erect, seized the Henry and the telescope, and ran to the end of the ridge. He scoured the land below but saw no hint of either Charlotte's men or Moon Killer's. Relieved, he returned to their camp and was about to shake Plumber when he saw something that filled him with dread.

Darlene's saddle and blankets were gone! Pivoting, Fargo discovered the bay was also missing. In the exact spot where Darlene had bedded down was her saddlebags, and lying on top of them was a flat sheet of paper with a small rock in the center to keep it from blowing away. Fargo quickly retrieved it.

"My darling Skye," the note began. "I apologize for deceiving you. I'm leaving now. I'm going to confront my destiny. To confront my sister. She has committed some vile deeds, it is true, but she is still family. I owe it to her, as well as to myself, to make one last effort to repair the rift between us. As Hiram put it, kin is always special. I must make the attempt even if it is doomed to fail."

Fargo swore. Her absence explained why she had drank so much coffee before going to bed. She'd never intended to fall asleep. He read on.

"Please don't be mad. It is something I must do, or I'll never be able to live with myself. Should the worst come to pass, please know that I will breathe my last thinking of your friendship. You are a very special man. In adoration, Darlene."

Crumbling the paper, Fargo walked to Hiram and stomped on his foot. Yipping like a snake-bit coyote, Plumber shot upright and looked around in confusion.

"What's wrong? Are we being attacked?"

"You fell asleep," Fargo growled.

"I tried not to. Honest! But I couldn't keep my eyes open." Hiram rubbed his stubble. "No harm done, though. We're alive and kicking."

"Darlene might not be for much longer," Fargo said, lifting his saddle and hastening to the stallion.

Hiram surveyed the immediate area. "Say, where the devil is Miss Weldon, anyhow? Her horse is gone."

"Nothing gets past you," Fargo responded not too kindly. Based on the tracks, Darlene had left hours ago, giving her more than ample time to find her sister. By now, Darlene might well be dead. Charlotte would have won. All his effort would have been for nothing.

"Why are you so mad?" Hiram quizzed. "You don't blame me, do you? Hell, I'd never have dozed off if I'd known this would happen."

"We're both to blame," Fargo said. Hiram, for falling asleep; him, for not realizing sooner how deeply troubled Darlene had been. He should have known she was up to something from the comments she'd made. "I'm going after her. Alone."

Hiram jumped to his feet. "Not on your life. You'll need an extra gun if you're tangling with that crowd."

Fargo refused to argue. "I won't tell you twice," he warned. Jezebel wouldn't be able to keep up with the Ovaro. And Hiram was as safe there as anywhere else. "Hide in the trees until I get back."

Plumber commenced muttering but Fargo ignored him

and hurriedly saddled up. Forking leather, Fargo reined the pinto around and trotted eastward, taking the slope at a reckless pace. Darlene's tracks were as plain as the new day. She had walked the bay for a while so as not to wake him and Hiram, then mounted and ridden off.

Someone once told Fargo that it was a woman's prerogative to change her mind. But Darlene went from one extreme to the other. First she'd fled Philadelphia in a panic, then she'd decided to resist Charlotte, and to do what was necessary to save herself. Now Darlene had changed her mind again, letting her feelings rule her instead of common sense, thinking with her heart instead of her head.

For Charlotte, it was a godsend. Darlene would ride right into her lap. All Charlotte had to do was say the word and any of her hired killers would cut Darlene down. Charlotte's problems were solved. She could return to Philadelphia, have the will nullified, and take over her father's estate, as simple as that.

Fargo should be mad at Darlene but he wasn't. She was misguided, mistaking guilt for affection. Out of a misplaced sense of loyalty she was throwing herself into the lion's den, as that parson in Yankton might say.

The bay's hoofprints pointed Fargo toward a dry wash not visible from the ridge. How Darlene had known where her sister's camp was mystified Fargo until he smelled smoke. Slowing, Fargo pulled out the Henry. It was rash to go on without reconnoitering. He reined up, slid off, and cat-footed nearer.

Darlene hadn't stopped. She'd boldly gone into the wash, and had ridden around a bend eighty feet away.

No lookouts were anywhere to be seen. Fargo went on, on foot. At the turn, a peek established that the wash extended for another sixty or seventy yards, passing a small hill. It was from the east side of the hill that the smoke rose. Wispy tendrils hovered about it like airborne serpents.

Fargo advanced, using the wash for cover until he was close enough to the hill to suit him. Slanting up and out, he relied on scattered brush and trees to screen him as he climbed midway to the top.

Crawling to where he could see what lay beyond, Fargo raised himself up on his elbows. Charlotte's camp was at the base of the hill, a little to the north. A coffeepot sat on a flat rock beside the fire. Close by were their tethered horses.

The four cutthroats Charlotte had hired were clustered together, doing the same thing Finlay and Gordon were doing; watching Charlotte Weldon torture her sister. Darlene was on her back, staked out spread-eagle, her fine dress smudged with dirt and badly torn. Circling her, holding a knife, was Charlotte.

Fargo's outrage knew no bounds when the redhead leaned over and jabbed the point of the blade into Darlene's exposed left leg. A red stain quickly spread. Gordon and several of the killers cackled as Charlotte, grinning savagely, did it again.

Ducking down, Fargo rose onto his hands and knees and angled higher, stopping when voices were audible. Wriggling to a high patch of weeds, he carefully parted them.

Charlotte was enjoying herself immensely. Wagging the bloody knife tip under her sister's nose, she taunted, "See this? This is what you deserve for being so stupid. Did you really think that all you had to do was appeal to my better nature and I'd change my ways?"

Darlene hadn't cried out. Nor did she answer now. Her silence infuriated Charlotte, who began beating her over the head and bosom with the knife's hilt, raising dark welts on Darlene's cheek and forehead.

Fargo leveled the Henry to fire, but just then Charlotte stopped.

"I want you to suffer!" the redhead screeched. "I want to see the agony in your eyes! To hear you plead for mercy!"

"Never!" Darlene spat. "I would die before I'd give you the satisfaction. If you're going to kill me, do it and be done with it."

Charlotte gripped the knife with both hands and raised it as if to thrust the razor-edged steel into her sister's chest, but she changed her mind at the last instant and lowered it. "No. That would be too easy on you."

Gordon was rubbing his hands in demented glee. "Poke out her eyes! Cut out her tongue!"

"Chop off her fingers and toes," one of the gunmen suggested. "I saw someone the Comanches did that to. They were begging to die."

Charlotte circled her sibling like a cat toying with a trapped mouse. "What to do, what to do? Until I decide, why don't I just let you bake in the sun? It will be blistering hot in another hour."

Darlene just wouldn't seem to learn. "I refuse to believe you're that wicked. Deep down you know this is wrong."

"Forget trying to save my soul. Your problem is saving your *life*."

Fargo spied a bronzed shape slinking toward the camp from the east and realized they all had a problem. In his worry for Darlene he had forgotten about the renegades. But Moon Killer hadn't forgotten about those his band had been shadowing. The renegades were closing in on them from three sides.

11

Skye Fargo counted twenty-two half-breeds from half-again as many tribes. By their features or their attire, he recognized one who was part Cheyenne, another who was part Arapaho, a third part Crow, and so on. Some were from tribes who were traditional enemies, yet they had banded together to kill under the common banner of mutual evil. An accident of birth had branded them outcasts, giving them a shared bond, wiping the slate clean of all past differences.

The renegades had fanned out in a crescent shape, one end of their line flanking the south side of the hill, and the other to the north. The only avenue of retreat for the whites would be up the slope, but Moon Killer was too clever to give Charlotte's bunch a chance to get away. His men were exercising extreme care. As stealthily as panthers, they crept toward their unsuspecting quarry.

At last Fargo saw the notorious Moon Killer in person. Moon Killer was a big man, though not exceptionally so, maybe two or three inches over six feet in height. What *was* exceptional was the renegade chieftain's head. The stories told about him were true. It was huge, unnaturally so, and almost perfectly round. It resembled nothing so much as an enormous pumpkin wedged onto human shoulders. Rendering it even more hideous were Moon Killer's thick, hairy eyebrows, his wide, flat nose, and oversized lips. Not only had he endured the shame of being born a breed, he had suffered the added indignity of being born deformed. His rabid spite for all whites and Indians alike took on a whole new meaning.

Moon Killer wore a loose buckskin shirt and baggy army pants—taken, no doubt, from a trooper he had slain. He wore a Smith & Wesson side arm and carried a Remington Rolling Block rifle, probably stripped from the hands of a dead white hunter. On his left hip in a beaded sheath was a bowie.

Fargo could see all of the renegades plainly, but Charlotte's band still had no idea they were about to be attacked. One of the rivermen had gone for coffee while his friend and the two gunmen ambled nearer to the women. Charlotte was pacing and pondering. Oddly enough, Darlene was calm, her lips moving as if she were praying.

Fargo was tempted to shout a warning, but it would do little good. The renegades were already close enough to pick the whites off with a volley or two, and random shots might hit Darlene. She was the only one he cared about. Charlotte deserved whatever befell her, while Finlay and Gordon . . . Fargo raised up a little higher. Where were they, anyway?

The two in question were moving toward the horses. Fargo saw Finlay glance sharply into the brush, then whisper something to Gordon. They were acting nonchalant, walking slowly and talking, but their ruse didn't fool Fargo. He could see they knew all about the renegades, yet they weren't alerting the others. Not even Charlotte.

It perplexed Fargo. Their sister was bound to die unless they got her out of there. Yet they didn't care. They were thinking only of their own miserable hides, saving themselves even if it meant sacrificing everyone else. They were as snake-low as two men could be and not have scales.

Charlotte stopped pacing. "Starkey!" she snapped at the gunman who wore two pistols strapped low on his hips. "Bring me a piece of firewood from out of the fire. I've had an inspiration."

As the gun shark walked off, his large Mexican-style

spurs jangling, Charlotte bent over her sister. "I've made up my mind, dear Darlene. Little by little I'm going to make a ruin of your lovely body, until there is nothing left but a quivering pile of bones and flesh. Your eyes, your fingers, your toes—you'll lose all of them. But slowly. Oh-so-slowly."

"You wouldn't."

Charlotte grabbed the front of Darlene's dress. "Haven't you gotten it through your head yet? I will stop at nothing to ensure the family fortune is mine. For years I've plotted. I stood at our father's elbow, learning all there is to know about the family's vast holdings so when I took them over, everything would run smoothly."

"Yet Father willed it all to me," Darlene said. "All your scheming was for naught."

A vicious backhand rocked her, and Charlotte drew back her hand to slap Darlene again. "Don't remind me! The fool! I'd proven myself to him. I'd shown that only *I* had what it takes to run the Weldon empire. I'm calculating and ruthless enough to succeed at anything I put my mind to."

"Father knew that," Darlene responded. "But he also knew there's one important quality you lack. He told me so himself. It must be why he left everything to me and not to you."

Charlotte's hand lowered. "What quality is that? What did he tell you?"

"Heart, Charlotte. He said you don't have any heart."

The redhead uncoiled, her features twisted like those of a feral beast. "Is that so?"

"Would I lie? He sat me down shortly before he became sick. He told me how disappointed he was in you. How he had hoped you would take over for him one day. But you don't have the heart for it, he said. You don't know there is a time for being kind as well as a time for being tough."

Charlotte was livid. "What does that have to do with running a business?" she snarled. "Too much emotion makes a person weak. Makes them vulnerable."

"I asked Father who would take over, then, if not you. I told him I had no interest in doing so. All he did was smile, pat my hand, and say that in time, everything would work out." Darlene closed her eyes in sorrow.

"You always were his little darling," Charlotte grated. Suddenly grabbing Darlene's hair, she shook her violently. "Too bad he can't see you now! Too bad he can't see what I'm going to do to his precious little angel."

Starkey returned bearing a length of dead branch, one end aflame. "Here you go, ma'am."

Charlotte snatched it and held it low, close to Darlene's head. "I'll start with your hair and work my way down. You've always been so proud of it."

Finlay and Gordon reached the horses. Without being obvious, they untied their animals. No one else other than Fargo noticed because the rivermen and gunmen were riveted on the two women.

They weren't the only ones. Twenty-two renegades were watching from concealment, and the most interested one of all appeared to be Moon Killer. He was on his knees behind some brush not twenty feet from Charlotte and Darlene. At a gesture, his men began to stalk forward. None raised a weapon.

That was when Fargo realized Moon Killer intended to take the whites alive. Torture was Moon Killer's specialty, and here were eight whites ripe for the taking. He wouldn't deprive himself of the pleasure of mutilating them, if he could help it. So what if it cost a few of his own men?

Fargo had no qualms about letting Charlotte Weldon fall into Moon Killer's clutches, not after what she had done to him. Darlene was another story. He wanted to spirit her to safety, but to do so, he must show himself. He must rush down the hill under the guns of the renegades, cut her loose, and somehow reach the Ovaro. But it just couldn't be done. There were too many of them.

So Fargo had to lie there, helpless, seething with frustration, as a fierce war whoop rent the air and a pack of bronzed wolves bounded from hiding, converging on their prey.

Charlotte whirled in consternation, the burning brand in her hand forgotten. The rivermen panicked and raced for their mounts. Finlay and Gordon swung up, reined their animals around, and made their break, riding pell-mell to the south.

Only the two gunmen fought back. A scarecrow packing a Whitney Navy pistol snapped off a single shot that dropped a charging foe. Then he was tackled by two other renegades and pinned to the ground.

That left the two guns of Starkey. He was whipcord lean and skilled with a pistol. Very skilled. His revolvers, nickel-plated Manhattans, were out in a twinkling. Double blasts from the .36-calibers dropped two half-breeds. Then, firing methodically, one pistol after the other, Starkey retreated toward the horses, bellowing, "Run, ma'am! I'll cover you!"

Charlotte came to life. Flinging the burning branch at a charging renegade, she turned and ran. But she hadn't taken four steps when Moon Killer himself was on her, springing like a cougar and pulling her down with him. Charlotte Weldon did something she had undoubtedly never done before: She screamed in mortal terror.

Starkey still had a chance to get away. A slim chance, but he was close enough to the horses to reach them. Instead, when Charlotte screamed, he headed toward her, his lethal revolvers dropping renegades with each crack. Six were down, dead or convulsing. It was too much for Moon Killer.

"Kill the son of a bitch!"

A dozen rifles fired in unison. Starkey staggered, ripped to tatters, yet he didn't drop. He fired at a renegade on his right, then dropped another on his left. Another second and his knees buckled, or he would have kept on firing. As he collapsed, he flung out his hands to catch himself. On hands and knees he looked up just as a renegade Cheyenne breed reached him. A heavy war club was lifted high.

The splat of the gunman's skull being split like a melon was loud enough for Fargo to hear.

Finlay and Gordon, meanwhile, were trying to break through the renegade cordon. They still clutched their canes, and the renegades, seeing that neither held a gun, rushed to intercept them and drag them from their saddles.

Fargo recalled Horace Plumber's last words: "Watch the canes! The canes!" Now he learned why. Finlay and Gordon jerked on the ivory handles and whipped glittering rapiers from mahogany scabbards. Galloping with their mounts shoulder to shoulder, the pair hurtled into the renegades like seasoned cavalry officers. They wielded their rapiers with devastating effect. Sunlight glistened off flashing steel. Two renegades fell in a torrent of scarlet. Then the brothers were in the clear and racing for their lives.

Moon Killer was furious. Holding Charlotte Weldon by the wrist, he bellowed orders. Four renegades dashed to the remaining horses, swiftly mounted, and gave chase. Two more ran into the brush to retrieve the band's own animals, Fargo suspected.

Of the renegades who had fallen, five were dead, the rest wounded, some only slightly. They gathered around the captives, who were stripped of weapons and herded together. The rivermen and the gunmen were as pale as sheets. Charlotte had recovered from her fear and stood with her chin high, her shoulders squared, glaring defiantly.

Moon Killer stepped over to Darlene. None of the renegades had touched her. Sinking onto a knee, he produced a knife and cut her loose with quick, sure strokes. As she sat up, he replaced the knife and reached out to touch her golden locks.

"Your hair, woman. It blazes like the sun."

Darlene pulled back, which was a mistake. Moon Killer seized her arm and brutally wrenched it, forcing her low to the ground.

"Pull away again and I'll gut you."

"I'm not scared of you!" Darlene responded, struggling.

Moon Killer was amused. Laughing, he yanked her erect and shoved her toward Charlotte and the others.

A swarthy warrior whose face was disfigured by a zigzagging scar that ran from above his right eye to below his chin walked up to the renegade leader. "Many die," he said gruffly. "Why we not kill white-eyes right off?"

Fargo was puzzled. Why were they speaking English? Then it dawned on him that with so many renegades, each from a different tribe and each speaking a different tongue, a smattering of English was the only language they might have in common, other than sign language.

Moon Killer faced the other. "I wanted them alive."

"Easier to kill them," the scarred man said. "Painted Pony now dead. Yellow Feather dead. For what?" He gestured in contempt at the captives.

The renegades closest to their leader began to back away. Some swapped worried looks. Fargo had heard that Moon Killer did not like to have his authority challenged, and he guessed what was coming.

"I say you were wrong," the malcontent continued to declare. "I say better to kill whites."

Moon Killer's great moon face creased into an evil grin. "You say? When did you take over?" Without warning, Moon Killer drove the barrel of his rifle into the other man's stomach, doubling him over. The scarred warrior staggered, his mouth agape. Moon Killer, his grin spreading, shoved the Remington's muzzle into the man's mouth and stroked the trigger.

None of the other renegades objected. They stared at the crumpled figure for a moment, then showed no more interest in him than they would a crushed fly.

Moon Killer turned to the whites. The rivermen and the gunman were trying to be brave, but their fidgeting betrayed their true state. Only Charlotte and Darlene showed no fear, Charlotte's eyes shooting lightning bolts at her captors. Darlene, resigned to the outcome, had her hands folded at her waist.

"Two white women." Moon Killer gloated. "Both beautiful." His tongue traced the outline of his sausage lips. "You are mine now to do with as I want."

"Go to hell, you heathen!" Charlotte declared. "I'd rather be skinned alive than have you grope me with your filthy paws."

To Fargo's surprise, the renegade chieftain didn't take offense. "You have fire. I like that. You will scratch and kick a lot, I think."

Darlene looked at him. "I won't. I won't resist at all."

"Either way is fine," Moon Killer said. He touched her tresses and this time she didn't recoil. "It shines," he said in fascination. "I have never seen hair like yours."

"Scalp her and you can keep it with you always," Charlotte said.

Several of the renegades laughed. Moon Killer's forehead creased as he glanced from one woman to the other. "You hate her, don't you? Why? What is she to you?"

"My sister."

Fargo could see that Moon Killer didn't know what to make of them. The butcher went to touch Charlotte's hair but she slapped his hand away. Instead of striking her, he leaned on his rifle.

"I saw you beat her. I saw you ready to burn her. Now you want me to lift your own sister's scalp? How can this be?"

"It's quite simple," Charlotte stated. "I hate her."

"Your own sister?" Moon Killer couldn't believe it.

Charlotte glared at Darlene. "I'd have done a lot worse to her if you hadn't interfered. She has plagued me since we were children, her and her noble ways. I want her dead, at any cost."

"She doesn't really mean it," Darlene said.

"Like hell I don't!" Charlotte screeched, and threw herself at Darlene, raking at her with her nails. Darlene, avoiding them, gripped her sister's wrists, and they grappled.

Most of the renegades thought it was hilarious, the two captives fighting like banshees. Moon Killer, though, was puzzled. He watched them roll back and forth, Charlotte pulling at Darlene's hair, Darlene vainly attempting to push her sister off. Then he jerked his right thumb and his men jumped to pry the women apart.

Charlotte resisted, hissing and kicking.

"Wildcats, these two, eh?" a member of the band said.

"I never see white women like these," mentioned another.

"Me neither," Moon Killer declared. "No one is to harm them. Whoever does, answers to me." Moon Killer waited for comments. There were none. "Tie their wrists. As for these other white-eyes"—he nodded at the rivermen and the gunman—"we have far to go. It is better to kill them here than take them along."

"Should we shoot them?" asked a man who was part Arapaho.

"And waste those stakes?" Moon Killer rejoined, pointing at the ones Darlene had been tied to. "We will amuse ourselves while we wait for Bull Elk to bring the other two whites back."

Fargo gazed to the south. Finlay and Gordon, and those after them, were well out of sight. A strident cry of horror signaled a commotion below as a river rat was dragged to his doom. He fought desperately but the renegades soon had him spread-eagled.

Moon Killer drew his bowie. "Come," he said to the women. "Watch what I do. Watch and learn."

Charlotte refused. "Sit on your knife, you savage. I'm not yours to be bossed around as you damn well please."

"Wrong," Moon Killer said.

The sisters, their wrists bound in front of them, were hauled close to the stakes and held so they couldn't avert their eyes. Moon Killer circled the whimpering riverman, made up his mind where to begin, and hunkered beside the hapless man's groin. Fargo couldn't quite see what Moon Killer did next, and an inhuman scream made him glad he couldn't. The riverman began to blubber hysterically as Moon Killer held up a piece of bloody flesh for the rest of the renegades to view.

Darlene sagged, close to fainting. The remaining riverman retched. The gunman closed his eyes and shuddered. Only Charlotte was unaffected, and when Moon Killer shook the dripping mass at her, she laughed.

Moon Killer rose. "I think I like you," he bluntly informed her. "You're not like other white women."

"A man after my own heart," Charlotte said, laughing louder. She sneered at Darlene.

"He's wicked. Unspeakably wicked," Darlene said.

"If so, then so am I," Charlotte said. "But you'll never admit the truth to yourself if you live to be a hundred. And do you know why?" Charlotte didn't let her sister answer. "Because if my blood is tainted, so is yours. You're not the paragon of virtue you pretend to be. If I can turn out like I have, then one day you might snap and become just like me."

Another ragged shriek from the victim drowned out whatever Darlene had said next. Fargo spotted the two renegades who had gone into the brush returning with the rest of the band's horses. He thought of trying to run the animals off, but in broad daylight it would be suicide. As much as it galled him, he simply had to face the fact there was nothing he could do for Darlene for the time being.

The first riverman did not last long. When Moon Killer was done with him, they brought the second one over. He resisted with all his might but they slammed him to the ground and bound him to the stakes. Moon Killer's bowie dipped, the riverman bawled, and Moon Killer held a bloody eyeball aloft.

"You're a monster!" Darlene exclaimed.

The renegade chieftain snickered along with Charlotte Weldon.

Fargo didn't watch the second riverman suffer the torment of the damned. His high-pitched wails were enough to scare off every bird and wild animal for a mile around. Moon Killer carved him up like a holiday turkey, a piece here, a piece there, cutting where it would hurt the most but never delivering a fatal stroke. Toward the end the man was in hysterics, pleading to be put out of his misery.

Next came the gunman. Moon Killer seemed to have been saving the most painful tortures for last. Excruciating beyond endurance, they soon reduced the gunman to a weeping wreck. Fargo was actually glad when the man's hair-raising screams were silenced by the final slash of the bowie across his throat.

Moon Killer was drenched in blood. Pressing a finger to a drop on his shirt, he licked the gore off and made a show of smacking his lips.

Loathing filled Fargo, a disgust such as he had rarely felt. All the tales he'd heard were true. Moon Killer was every bit the abomination people had painted him. Fargo would dearly love to put a slug into the man's disfigured pumpkin head but he couldn't yet, for Darlene's sake.

The renegades began to go through the packs Charlotte's party had brought, keeping whatever struck their fancy. One put on a dress and pranced around. Another was partial to Charlotte's hat with the bobbing peacock feather.

Noon came, and still the men Moon Killer had sent after Finlay and Gordon didn't show. Moon Killer prowled the camp like a surly bear, cuffing anyone who didn't do his bidding fast enough to suit him.

Charlotte and Darlene had been dumped near the fire. They were offered coffee and biscuits, but they refused.

By the position of the sun, Fargo saw that it was one o'clock when Moon Killer finally gave the order to mount up. The leader climbed onto his Appaloosa and rose in the stirrups. "We have waited long enough. Bull Elk will track us and catch up." With a wave of his arm, the band thundered to the northeast. The bodies of the whites and the slain renegades were left for scavengers to devour.

Fargo lost no time in reaching the Ovaro. Keeping the band in sight without being seen was easy thanks to the telescope.

The renegades rode until dark. At the base of a low, isolated bluff they picketed their horses, posted guards, and settled down for the night.

Fargo drew rein half a mile off and spied on them for an hour before venturing closer. Evidently Moon Killer had chosen the spot because of a spring. The men took turns leading their mounts to drink, then the provisions belonging to Charlotte were opened and supper was prepared.

The aroma of boiling coffee and sizzling bacon made Fargo's stomach growl. He'd not eaten all day. From behind a boulder he saw Moon Killer take a seat beside the fire. Both women were brought over and shoved to their knees. Darlene bowed her head but Charlotte was as defiant as ever.

"If you're going to murder us, get it over with. I'm tired of being treated like one of your squaws."

Moon Killer speared his bowie into a pan, flicked a slice of bacon to his mouth, and chewed noisily. "Maybe I won't kill either of you. How would that be?"

"Why so generous?" Charlotte asked.

"For a man to have a woman with hair like the sun is good medicine," Moon Killer said, his oval chin bobbing at Darlene. "Powerful medicine."

Charlotte was never one to bandy words. "And me?"

Moon Killer lanced another bacon strip and held it out for her to take. "You remind me of myself. We are much alike, woman. We put ourselves before all else. And we do what we must to get what we want."

"I suppose I should be flattered." Charlotte accepted the morsel and took a bite.

"Most white women are not like you," Moon Killer said.

"They are weak. Puny. Worthless. The last one I caught was a log in bed. She did not give me pleasure so I had her breasts cut off. I made tobacco pouches out of them." He licked the tip of his bowie clean of bacon juice. "I hope you will do better."

"And if I refuse?"

"I will rape you. After I rape your sister."

So there it was. Fargo had only enough time until they turned in to think of a way to get Darlene out of there. Saving her from ordinary Indians would be hard enough. From the renegades, it would be twice as difficult, as they were twice as wary and twice as deadly.

Darlene was offered some bacon but she shook her head. "I would rather starve. After the atrocities I witnessed today, I can safely say you're the most despicable human being on the face of the planet."

Moon Killer uncoiled, his free hand whipping against Darlene's cheek, spilling her onto her side. Clamping his fingers onto her jaw, he pressed the bowie knife to her throat. "Listen well, woman. You live only so long as I say you live. Hair or no hair, do not insult me again."

Charlotte jumped up. "Do it! Go ahead!"

Fargo tensed. It wouldn't take much for the renegade to lose his temper completely. He prayed Darlene would keep quiet but he should have known better.

"Did I say despicable? That's too tame. You're an abomination, Moon Killer. A brute and a bully and a coward, all rolled into one. So kill me! I dare you!"

12

Skye Fargo held his breath almost as long as he had when he was at the bottom of the Missouri River. The Henry was squarely centered on Moon Killer's great head, but coring the butcher's brain might cause his arm to spasm. The bowie would end up buried in Darlene's throat. So Fargo waited, holding his breath to steady his aim, only willing to fire as a last resort.

Charlotte, prancing like a crazed goat, urged the renegade leader on. "Do it! Do it! Kill her now!"

Moon Killer glanced in annoyance at the redhead, then looked at Darlene and lowered his knife. "Not yet."

Forgetting herself, Charlotte grabbed his arm. "What's the matter with you? I thought we were kindred souls. Bleed her, damn you!"

Growling like a grizzly, Moon Killer slapped Charlotte four times in swift succession. "No one tells me what to do! *No one!*" Seizing her by her bound wrists, he threw her to the ground and kicked at her. "I will decide when it is time. Not you, you white cur." Moon Killer reversed his grip on the bowie and raised it, about to bash her with the hilt.

Charlotte glared, unafraid, as vicious in her way as he was in his. "If you expect me to grovel, forget it. I don't eat crow."

The flush of fury faded from the leader's round face. Moon Killer jerked the knife down, then placed a hand on Darlene's head. "Your golden hair has saved you again.

Tonight I want to make love to you, and I can't do that if you are dead."

"You won't enjoy it," Darlene said. "I'll see to that."

"Then I will finish what I started," Moon Killer promised, "and keep your scalp, as your sister begs me to do."

Charlotte was sitting up. "I hope I'm alive to see that. I could go to my grave happy." Brushing dirt from her riding outfit, she smiled crookedly at the man who had just savagely beaten her. "I'd even reward you as you've never been rewarded before."

"I have no use for the white man's money," Moon Killer said.

"And I wasn't offering any," Charlotte countered. "My reward would be a night under the blankets you would never forget."

Moon Killer sank back down, cross-legged. "You are the only person I have ever met who hates as much as I do. Yet you are female."

"So? Women can be just as ruthless as men. More so, when we put our minds to it." Charlotte smiled seductively. "You should keep me around. I can be of help to you."

"Earlier you did not want me to touch you," Moon Killer reminded her. "Now you throw yourself at me. Why the change?"

"For the man who kills my sister, I would do anything."

Charlotte wasn't fooling anyone, Fargo reflected, least of all the renegade. She thought that she could win Moon Killer over with her wiles and her charm, and at some point an opportunity to escape would arise. But she was in for a nasty shock. Moon Killer would let her live only so long as it suited him. When he tired of her, he would snuff out her life as casually as he'd snuff out a candle.

The rest of the band did not show much interest in what their leader was up to. Most were huddled around a couple of other small fires, as was Indian custom. They were eating and drinking and telling tales. Three warriors had been posted at the camp's perimeter, while two more were on guard by the string of horses. Moon Killer hadn't survived as long as he had by being careless.

The sentries compounded Fargo's problem. He gauged the distance between them, noting shadowed areas where a man might crawl into the camp unseen. The horses were close to the base of the bluff, the warriors guarding them at the middle of the string instead of at either end. It gave him an idea.

Folding his arms, Fargo rested his chin on his wrists. It would be a couple of hours yet before Moon Killer turned in for the night. Fargo could spare an hour to allow the sentries time to grow bored and a little less alert.

Moon Killer was shoveling bacon into his mouth and snorting like a hog at a trough when a Crow warrior came over carrying saddlebags.

"I found three of these." The man held up a book. "What do I do with them? Burn them?"

"Those are mine!" Darlene declared, scrambling to her knees. She lunged but the Crow snatched the volume away. "Give them to me!"

Moon Killer stopped chomping and extended a greasy palm for the Crow to place the book in his hand. "I have not yet learned to read the tracks whites make on paper. What is this? The white holy book I hear so much about?"

"No, it's one of my poetry books," Darlene said.

"Poetry? What is that?"

"You've never heard a poem? Allow me." Darlene took the leather-bound volume in both hands and flipped to the first page. "This is 'Don Juan' by my favorite poet, Lord Byron." Darlene cleared her throat and began reading. " 'I would to heaven that I were so much clay, as I am blood, bone, marrow, passion, feeling, because at least the past were passed away. And for the future—but I write this reeling, having got drunk exceedingly today—' "

Moon Killer laughed. "He got drunk? I like this poetry of yours. Read to me while I eat. It will amuse me."

Darlene was all too willing to oblige. Her melodious

voice carried far, her rich, musical lilt turning every head. Soon every last renegade was fixed on her in rapt attention. Even the sentries and the horse guards moved closer to hear.

Fargo could scarcely credit his own eyes. The most bloodthirsty butcher in the territory and his equally murderous minions were captivated by a *poem*? What made it even more remarkable was that he doubted they understood all the words. Some of the words even he hadn't heard before. But Darlene had the cutthroats mesmerized.

Rising, Fargo glided to the left. She had inadvertently given him a golden opportunity and he wasn't going to waste it. With all the renegades distracted, there would be no better time to attempt a rescue.

Like a buckskin-clad specter, Fargo passed within twenty feet of a sentry without being spotted. He circled wide toward the north end of the bluff, and when he was abreast of the horse string he dropped onto his stomach. Holding the Henry in his left hand, Fargo crawled along a narrow belt of inky darkness to within a few yards of the mounts. Slowing, he studied them closely. Several had caught his scent or had heard him. Their nostrils were flared, their ears were pricked. A single loud whinny would give him away.

In a crouch, Fargo crept up to the first animal and stroked its neck. When the others saw he wasn't a threat, they lowered their heads again.

A long rope had been slung between a stunted tree and a boulder, and each horse had been tied to it. Fargo moved down the line, unwrapping their reins, freeing them one by one. He was midway when a mare he was untying nickered lightly. One of the guards turned, and Fargo froze.

The guard wore a wide-brimmed black hat and knee-high moccasins. He took a step, his dark eyes narrowing, but Darlene's voice drew him back again. Giving the string a quick scrutiny, he turned and went on listening to her.

Fargo patted the mare and finished untying her, and then the rest. At the far end he found Moon Killer's big Appaloosa, which suited his purpose just fine. Holding on to its reins, he rubbed its neck, and when he was sure it wouldn't act up, he swung a leg up and over the mount.

None of the renegades were looking his way. Fargo turned the Appaloosa, then raised the Henry. In a few seconds all hell would break loose; he mustn't lose track of Darlene. Keeping her in sight, he banged off three shots and let out with a war whoop that would do a Chiricahua Apache justice. The horses broke and ran, wheeling in a body and fleeing in the only direction open to them—straight at the renegades.

Fargo fired again and whooped some more as he slapped his legs against the Appaloosa, joining the horses in their flight. Shouts and curses were added to the bedlam as the renegades leaped up. Some scurried for safety. Others attempted to stop the stampede.

Moon Killer was roaring orders, but no one heeded. Charlotte and Darlene were also on their feet, rooted by surprise.

In a burst of speed Fargo hurtled past most of the horses. He saw several beasts nearly trample the women. One clipped Darlene, almost knocking her down. Fargo veered toward her, calling out her name, but she didn't hear him over the din of thundering horses.

Someone else did, though. Moon Killer bellowed like a bull and snatched up his rifle. Jamming it against his shoulder, the butcher fired at the exact instant Fargo did. A leaden hornet buzzed by Fargo's ear. His shot jolted Moon Killer, but the scourge of the plains didn't drop. They both fired a second time. Only Fargo fired a third. For by then Moon Killer was oozing like melted wax to the ground, two new holes in his great moon face, smack between the eyes.

"Darlene!" Fargo hollered, switching the Henry to his right hand and leaning down with his left arm outstretched. "Catch hold!"

"Skye!" Darlene took a few running steps and threw herself at him.

Fargo snagged her on the fly, his arm wrapping around her slim waist. Confusion reigned on all sides, with horses streaking into the night, renegades vainly seeking to stop their panicked flight. A few shots rang out but none came close. Within moments the Appaloosa was beyond the firelight, and Fargo shifted to swing Darlene on behind him.

"Wait!" she cried. "My sister! We have to go back!"

"Nothing doing," Fargo responded.

Darlene gripped his shoulders. "Please, Skye! Please!"

Against his better judgment, Fargo hauled on the reins and looked back. A cloud of dust shrouded most of the renegades. A few had caught horses but the animals reared and plunged. Seven or eight warriors were gathered around Moon Killer's corpse in confusion.

"Where is she?" Darlene asked, worried sick.

From out of the dust came Charlotte. She was coughing and limping, favoring her right leg. Spying them, she waved her bound arms. "Wait! Don't leave me! Please, Darlene! I beg you!"

Darlene started kicking the Appaloosa. "Turn around, damn it! We've got to save her! Hurry! Before they see her!"

The renegades already had. A ragged volley echoed off the bluff. Charlotte Weldon pitched forward, stumbled, and fell to one knee, her riding outfit riddled with lead. Weakly, she sought to rise, a second volley smashing her to the dirt, where she twitched a few times and then was still.

"Noooooo!" Darlene wailed. Pushing against Fargo, she tried to jump down. But Fargo wouldn't let her. Holding fast, he spurred the Appaloosa to a gallop. Renegades were running to cut them off, firing as they ran, their bullets clipping the brush on both sides. Darlene, weeping, abruptly collapsed against him.

"Are you hit?" Fargo yelled.

"My sister!" Darlene sobbed. "My poor sister!"

The Appaloosa soon outdistanced any pursuit but Fargo didn't slow down again until they reached the Ovaro.

Switching to the stallion, he held on to the Appaloosa's reins and resumed their flight. By his reckoning it would take the renegades most of the night to gather their mounts, and he didn't think any would bother to give chase. With Moon Killer dead, they would disperse or go into hiding to pick a new leader.

The worst was over. All that remained was for Fargo to get Hiram Plumber and head for Yankton.

For over an hour Darlene quietly wept. The back of Fargo's shirt was damp from her tears when she stopped sniffling and sat up. "Charlotte is gone. I feel so alone, so empty inside."

In Fargo's estimation she should feel happy. Now she could return to Philadelphia, and the judge would appoint her the rightful heir. Millions of dollars would fall in her lap. A life of luxury awaited her, a life most people could only dream about.

All night they rode, arriving at the ridge as dawn birthed a new day. Darlene had fallen asleep, slumped against Fargo's broad back. She awoke as he drew rein beside the ring of rocks he had built to screen their fire. It had long since died out.

"Hiram?" Fargo shouted.

Jezebel and her owner were nowhere around.

"Where can he be?" Darlene asked. "Could those awful men have gotten hold of him and we didn't know it?"

"No." Fargo rose in the stirrups. "Hiram! Where the hell are you?" Climbing down, he rekindled the fire and put coffee on to brew. It had been a full twenty-four hours since he slept last and he'd need to drink a gallon in order to stay sharp. While Darlene fussed with her hair and dress, he prowled the woods for sign. Tracks revealed that Hiram had led Jezebel into the trees, as he'd been told to do, but he hadn't stayed more than a couple of hours. The mule's hoofprints pointed toward Yankton.

Darlene was wiping her face with a strip torn from the

sleeve of her dress when Fargo strode back out from the undergrowth. "Did you find him?"

"He's on his way to town. We'll rest until noon and follow him." Fargo tested the coffee by brushing a finger across the pot. It wasn't quite hot enough.

"Can we catch up?"

Hiram had too much of a start, and Fargo said so. Fishing the bundle of pemmican from his saddlebags, he gave some to Darlene. She didn't eat much. Sitting there with her hands clasped across her chest and her knees pressed tight, she gazed forlornly out over the countryside.

Fargo wisely made no mention of Charlotte. He spread out his blankets and gestured for Darlene to lie down. "Get some rest. I'll wake you in three or four hours."

"What about you? You must be as tired as I am."

"I'll manage." Fargo would catch up on his sleep when he was certain beyond a shadow of a doubt that the renegades weren't after them. Night would fall soon enough.

Hardly had Darlene laid down than she was asleep. Fargo walked to the rim with her telescope to scour their back trail. No riders or dust clouds were evident. Bubbling sounds from the coffeepot brought him back to the fire, and he downed four brimming cups in a row.

The sun seemed to take forever to reach its zenith. Fargo gently roused Darlene, who resisted waking up. She was as sluggish as a snail as she rose and smoothed her badly rumpled clothes.

"So soon? It feels as if I just fell asleep." Darlene stretched. "When we reach town I'm crawling into bed and staying there for a week. Then I'm soaking in a tub until I'm as wrinkled as a prune. What about you?"

"A thick steak and a bottle of whiskey will do just fine," Fargo said. That, and another night with Sally Crane. Afterward, it would be off to Denver and the high Rockies.

Darlene grinned. "We could soak in the tub together."

She was inviting him to do more than take a bath, and they both knew it. Fargo filled his tin cup and gave it to her.

"There are a lot of places I haven't been to yet, a lot of sights I haven't seen."

"Well, if you ever change your mind, Philadelphia isn't hard to find."

An awkward silence claimed them. In half an hour they were on the move again. The Appaloosa was growing accustomed to Darlene and gave her no trouble. By late afternoon they were crossing rolling hills, Fargo in the lead. As he came over the crest of the next one, he saw buzzards circling above a basin below.

"Do you think it's Hiram?" Darlene asked.

Fargo investigated. The vultures were gorging on a rare feast. Not Plumber and the mule, as Fargo feared, but on the bodies of four renegades, the four Moon Killer had sent after Finlay and Gordon. Taking reluctant wing as Fargo and Darlene approached, the ungainly carrion eaters flapped low overhead, waiting for the pair who had intruded on their meal to leave.

Darlene held back, appalled at the bloated, bloody forms. "How did this happen?"

Fargo would like to know himself. Finlay and Gordon hadn't impressed him as being formidable fighters, yet they had broken through the renegade line and slain the warriors sent after them. Scores of puncture wounds proved it was the brothers' handiwork. Yet how had they lured the warriors in close enough to use their rapiers?

Jezebel's tracks led to the bodies, circled to the left, and continued on. Fargo spurred the stallion after her. From the mule's stride, Fargo could see that Hiram had been in no great hurry. Maybe, Fargo mused, they'd catch up to him after all.

On the far side of the basin were more tracks made by a pair of shod horses. "Finlay and Gordon," Fargo said aloud. The brothers were making for the James River, and Hiram was unwittingly taking the same route.

"They're still alive?" Darlene was horrified. "Then it's not over. I'm no safer now than I was before."

Another three miles brought them to a strip of forest. As Fargo threaded through the trees he caught a whiff of an odor he hadn't smelled since his last visit to Arizona. It grew stronger, and he motioned for Darlene to halt. "Wait for me to holler," he said, shucking the Henry from the saddle scabbard.

Fargo only had to go another thirty yards. A haunch of mule meat on a makeshift spit was roasting over crackling flames. Nearby lay what was left of Jezebel. She had been stabbed again and again, just like the renegades, just like Amanda and Horace Plumber.

A groan snapped Fargo's head up. Across the clearing was Hiram, tied to a tree, the front of his shirt stained with blood. Fargo vaulted down and ran over. The only wound was high on Hiram's shoulder, a thin hole made by a rapier. There was also a large bump on the back of his head.

To the right of Fargo's position, a twig snapped and he spun, leveling the Henry, but it was only the two horses, tethered to limbs. Pivoting on the heel of his boot, he started to go get Darlene rather than shouting after her. The brothers had to be nearby and would hear. But she was already there—and so were Finlay and Gordon.

They stood on either side of her, each with a gleaming blade poised to plunge into her neck. Their fancy suits, high hats, and polished shoes were almost comical in the wilderness, as out of place as a mountain lion would be in New York City. Yet there was no denying they were every bit as deadly.

"Well, well. What have we here, brother?" Gordon said. "Another guest for supper?"

Finlay pressed the tip of his rapier to Darlene's skin. "Throw your rifle into the weeds behind you, Mr. Fargo. Then do the same with your gunbelt." He pricked Darlene, and she flinched. "Do it slowly or this lovely lady's death will be on your conscience."

It was no idle threat. Fargo did exactly as he was instructed, then hiked his arms over his head. He wanted to beat his head against a tree for being taken so easily. Like a rank greenhorn, he had blundered into their snare.

Darlene's eyes were moist. "I'm sorry," she said softly. "They jumped me and pulled me off my horse. There was nothing I could do."

"Not if she wanted to live." Gordon gloated. "For a while, at least." Lowering his rapier, he strutted around the fire. "Admit it, friend. You never figured on seeing us again, did you?"

Fargo had to stall. Somehow, he must draw Finlay away from Darlene. "We found the four renegades. You were lucky."

Gordon chortled. "Luck had nothing to do with it, you pathetic hick. I pretended to be dead, with my cane sword under me. My brother was hiding in the high grass. When those simple-minded savages climbed down to turn me over, we sprung our little surprise."

"And him?" Fargo said, nodding at Plumber.

"The fool saw our fire and came riding right into our camp." Gordon laughed. "We didn't know who he was at first. Then he started talking about how he was helping a blond lady by the name of Weldon."

Only then did Fargo recall that Hiram had never set eyes on the brothers before. "So you stabbed him and hit him over the head."

"You've got it backwards," Gordon said. "Finlay hit him, *then* I stabbed him." Gordon swung his rapier in a smooth flourish. "I like the feel of cold steel sliding into flesh. Once I start, I can't seem to stop."

"You would." Fargo was becoming worried. Finlay hadn't moved. "So it was you who made pin cushions of the renegades and the mule?"

"None other," Gordon said with a mock bow. He poked his blade into the carcass's haunch. "We were starving, and your friend mentioned how delicious some find mule meat to be." Gordon smacked his lips. "Indeed, it's not bad at all." He tilted the rapier toward Fargo. "But enough talk.

Now it's your turn. My darling cousin gets to see you die before she does. Isn't that considerate of me?"

Fargo faced Finlay, across the fire. "What about you? Are you willing to stand by while she's stabbed to death?"

"My dear fellow," Finlay said suavely. "I'll help him. What is her life compared to the fortune my brother and I will reap? We ran out on Charlotte when she needed us most because we wanted her to die. Just as we do Darlene. With them out of the way, we have a legitimate right to the fortune."

"You intended to kill both sisters all along?" Fargo edged his right foot forward so his boot was almost in the flames.

"Of course. Oh, we went along with Charlotte for as long as it was necessary. Our original plan was to be on hand when she murdered Darlene, then turn her in to the authorities." Finlay lowered his weapon a few inches. "But events worked out even better for us."

Gordon adopted a fencing stance. "Once we've disposed of the two of you, our worries are over."

"Never count your chickens before they're hatched," Fargo said. As he spoke, he kicked his boot into the fire, sending a shower of burning wood, flames, and smoke at Finlay, who sprang away from Darlene.

Fargo spun, dodging Gordon's rapier, and tried to seize Gordon's wrist. But the younger brother nimbly slipped from his grasp. Again the rapier flashed, directly at Fargo's eye. Ducking, he drove his right fist into Gordon's groin, then retreated a step and crouched, his hand dropping to the sheath on his right ankle.

To Gordon it must have appeared as if Fargo stumbled. "Die, you bastard!" he fumed, thrusting for a quick kill.

Fargo only had to shift a few inches to avoid the shearing blade. His arm rose in an arc, the Arkansas toothpick slicing into Gordon just below the jaw.

Gordon jerked backward, taking the toothpick with him. Scarlet gushed over his lower lip as he pivoted, reaching for his brother, who was rushing around the fire. Gordon fell into Finlay's arms, convulsed wildly for a moment, and died.

Fargo swung toward the weeds, searching for his guns. Darlene's shouted warning saved his life as an enraged Finlay Weldon attacked with the fury of a berserk wolverine. The rapier weaved a glittering tapestry of lunges, cleaves, and stabs. Fargo dodged, twisted, and whirled, always in motion, always one step ahead of the streaking steel. But Finlay was a master swordsman and it would be only a matter of seconds before he ran Fargo through.

They reached the weeds. Fargo skipped to the left, the rapier sizzling past his ear. Finlay set himself, and smiled. His next stroke would be fatal. Then, just by Fargo's feet, he found the Colt. Diving, Fargo palmed it. The rapier was spearing toward his heart when Fargo snapped off a shot that flung Finlay backward. Finlay sprang again, only to be met by hot lead that felled him in his tracks.

Fargo stared at the brothers a moment, then shoved his smoking Colt into his holster. He turned to cut Plumber loose but Darlene flew into his arms and hugged him close, her tears of joy trickling down his neck.

"I'm finally safe?"

"You're safe," Fargo said.

To spare Hiram the grisly sight of Jezebel's remains, Fargo quickly slashed the rope and boosted him onto the Ovaro. Later they would bandage his shoulder, and by morning they would be in Yankton. Where it had all begun.

Fargo could taste that steak already.

*1861, New Mexico Territory—where the fiercest
winds and the fastest guns are no match
for a woman spurned. . . .*

A bad wind blew from the north, shrieking across the desolate plains like a soul in torment, and driving hard pellets of frozen snow before it. It seemed to be trying to dislodge a lone rider from his saddle.

The man was big, though, and strong. He was also tough as old whitleather and wise to the ways of both wind and man. He sat his big pinto stallion stubbornly, refusing to give in to the gale. He hunched over, attempting to give the forceful wind a smaller target. The man was Skye Fargo, and he planned on getting to Spanish Bend, wind or no wind, snow or no snow.

Sleet stung the few bare patches of skin it could find on Fargo's face. He'd tied his hat down with a woolen muffler, and had a bandanna pulled over his nose and mouth. Both were now frozen solid. Fargo was pretty cold himself, in spite of the heavy leggings and sheepskin-lined jacket he wore.

His hands, encased in thick gloves, felt like blocks of ice. At this point, he wasn't altogether sure he could pry them free from the reins gripped tightly in his fingers if he had to.

Before the snow began, Fargo had watched a herd of antelopes foraging for grass on the winter-bare plains. Now even those few scrubby bunches of withered grama grass were buried under piles of snow, and his mind's eye pictured the antelopes, discouraged, bent against the howling wind just as he was.

He'd wondered before how those poor creatures managed to live out here. Even when the weather was fair, the pickings were slim in southeastern New Mexico Territory. He'd have thought any animal with a brain would have sought greener pastures. Not the pronghorns. Tough customers, those antelopes. Fargo admired their grit. He preferred to think of them as courageous rather than brainless. Under the circumstances, he feared he himself might be the brainless one.

He slouched farther over the Ovaro's back and cursed himself when the horse stumbled on something neither of them could see for the snow covering it. Fargo was a little worried about the harsh weather, although both he and his horse had been through worse conditions together. Not often, however, and seldom in such barren country.

It was impossible to see where he was going, and it was impossible to judge directions, even though he possessed a well-deserved reputation as a brilliant frontiersman. For all he knew, in spite of his years as a trailblazer in the wilderness, he and the Ovaro might be traveling around in slow circles.

He pictured that in his mind's eye too: him and his horse, floundering around and around until the snow stopped. Or until they froze into solid chunks, thus providing sustenance for any hungry coyotes in the neighborhood. No buzzards, though. The buzzards were wintering in Mexico. Smart birds, those buzzards, Fargo thought.

The truly bad weather never lasted long in these parts. It did its dirty work fast and went away again. There were no nine-month winters in southeastern New Mexico Territory. Winters out here usually came in treacherous patches that snuck up on a man and attacked him when his back was turned.

Nevertheless, Fargo knew it had been foolhardy of him to set out across these bleak plains when he'd known good and well a winter storm was brewing, and that he'd never get all the way to Spanish Bend before it hit. The land in these parts was hard, even when a body could see it. When it was covered with snow, as it was now, a horse might break a leg in a prairie-dog hole, walk into any number of needle-spiked cacti, or blunder into a snow-buried mesquite or greasewood plant. Fargo assumed his horse had just done the latter.

He peered through wind blown snow flurries at a steel gray sky, and cursed himself again. The bareness of these plains made the wind seem especially bitter. There was nothing to stop it except the occasional idiot who ventured outdoors when it blew. Today he was the idiot, and he didn't like knowing it.

The only reason he'd done such a damnfool thing was because he'd been so worried by Kitty's letter. Hell, he'd known Kitty O'Malley forever, and he was as fond of her as he was of anyone. He'd met her in San Antonio, but the letter had been posted from the little town of Spanish Bend where, so she'd written, she'd opened a saloon. He'd planned to pay Kitty a visit anyway, but he'd aimed to do it when the weather was better.

Now, however, according to her letter, Kitty was in trouble, and Fargo aimed to help her get out of it. Since the trouble sounded both serious and urgent, he'd left the security of Fort Sumner in spite of the huge black clouds piled up in the north, and a wind as sharp as knives. He'd done so, against all of his frontier knowledge and survival instincts, for the sake of an old and dear friend.

"We'll be all right, boy," he assured the Ovaro, hoping he was right. If he managed to get himself killed, so be it. It was the chance he took every day of his life. But if he got his horse killed, he was an ass. Skye Fargo would rather put himself in jeopardy than his trusted mount, but oftentimes, like now, it couldn't be helped.

The sleet had thickened, and snow began falling hard and fast, almost horizontally now, thanks to the wind. Fargo estimated it was blowing a good twenty-five or thirty miles an hour. Faster than a train could move, for the love of God. He looked up again, hoping to perceive any kind of a hint that the weather might break soon. There was none. They were in for it, with no respite in sight. Damn.

Fargo didn't know how long he'd been in the saddle, getting stiffer and colder and wondering how long he and his horse could last, when the smell of wood smoke permeated the freezing air and his stiff bandanna. Hardly daring to believe it, his eyes opening wide in surprise and hope, he sniffed again.

It was definitely smoke from a wood fire. Sweet Lord have mercy, maybe there was some kind of life out here after all. He'd thought he'd have to ride clear to Spanish Bend before he and the Ovaro could thaw out.

Cheered considerably, Fargo guided the pinto through the heavy drifts. He did so carefully, and not merely because of the foul weather. While he didn't fancy freezing to death, he also didn't fancy getting shot. It wasn't only the landscape out here that was rough. The people who lived on it were often even rougher. They had to be.

"There it is, boy."

Squinting through the white veil of falling snow, Fargo could barely make out the glowing smear of a candlelit window. Snow muffled the sound of the Ovaro's hooves, but Fargo approached the window warily. A few yards farther along he distinguished a dark bump rising from the snow like a monster out of a childhood nightmare. Squinting harder, he thought he could make it out as one small, lonely structure. It was more of a cabin than a house, he decided after another few moments of scrutiny. Smoke poured from the cabin's chimney, and was absorbed into the gray sky.

"It's not much of a place."

That was all right with Fargo. Any billet at all would be welcome at this point. He hoped there would be a barn or some kind of shelter for the Ovaro.

Few trees grew out here on the high plains, and those that did were stunted and had been shaped into low-growing, contorted forms by the eternal wind. Fargo had nothing behind which to conceal himself as he neared the cabin. His senses on the alert, he took off his right glove, tried to flex his fingers a few times, and drew his Colt. He trusted that if there were unfriendly gunmen inside, they were huddled around a fire and not expecting visitors.

He slowly circled the cabin on the Ovaro, which had a hard go of it through the deep drifts. Fargo was searching for any signs that the cabin's inhabitants might be hostile. There weren't any. He did, however, find a tumble-down barn. He considered this a good omen, since it ensured his horse shelter from the storm. And him, too, if whoever was inside that cabin wouldn't let him in.

Since snow had covered any tracks that might have been left by other cattle entering or leaving the barn, Fargo dismounted. His legs sank in a drift up to his knees, and his march to the barn's door was slow and laborious. When he finally got there, he stood aside and pushed the door open. Its hinges screeched like seventeen untuned fiddles. Fargo winced at the noise, and flattened himself against the side of the barn.

After the squealing of hinges quieted, the only thing that greeted him was silence and cavernous darkness. The eerie stillness lasted for several seconds before it was broken by the loud braying of a mule.

Fargo had been prepared for a shower of bullets.. He wouldn't have been surprised by a fist in the face. The mule's sudden, unexpected "hee-haw" made him jump nearly out of his skin.

Almost simultaneously, he heard a window being pushed open, and a woman calling, "Who's out there? Show yourself, or I'll shoot." Fargo decided luck was truly on his side today. He'd recognize that voice anywhere. It belonged to Kitty O'Malley.

Relieved, he called back, "It's me, Kitty. Skye Fargo."

"Skye! Oh, Skye! You came!"

She sounded as if she'd been crying, which was unlike Kitty, who was at least as tough as nails and generally as cheerful as a bird. He frowned, not bothering to holster his Colt. "You alone in there, Kitty?"

"Except for a friend of mine, Sally Brown. You don't know her. Oh, Skye, I've needed you so bad!"

Good God, she *was* crying. Fargo was appalled. "Be right there. Got to take care of my horse."

"Hurry. Please hurry, Skye." Kitty sniffled loudly and slammed the window shut.

Unsettled by Kitty's obvious distress, Fargo entered the barn, being careful in case anyone might be lurking inside. The only thing in the barn was the mule, though, and it brayed again.

The coast was clear, so he reholstered his Colt and slid

his glove over his nearly frozen fingers. Lord, he'd be glad to get inside and sit beside that fire with Kitty. She'd always been able to warm him up in the past in more ways than one. Too bad she had a friend with her. On the other hand, maybe this Sally Brown character was as friendly as Kitty. He felt warmer already.

The Ovaro didn't mind companionship either, so the Trailsman had no compunction about stabling him next to the noise maker. There were even some oats in a barrel.

Fargo gave his horse a good meal and some water, brushed him down, spread a blanket over him, and headed out of the barn. The wind almost yanked the door out of his hand, but he was able to get it shut again with a struggle. The snow and wind had worsened into a regular blizzard, and he was mortally glad he'd discovered the cabin, especially since it was Kitty's. He was also glad the sun, if it was there, hadn't set yet. It was already almost too dark to see, and it couldn't be much past noon. Come nighttime, it would be black as pitch outdoors and too dangerous to travel, even for him.

Before he'd reached the door, Kitty had flung it open and barreled outside and into his arms. She was as warm as toast against his frozen body.

She leaped back almost as soon as she touched him. Fargo was disappointed.

"Shoot, Skye, you're freezing."

"You're t-telling me." He walked stiff-legged into the room. Kitty closed the door behind him. "Lord, Skye, you look like an icicle."

Fargo didn't suppose the cabin would feel awfully warm to anyone who wasn't half frozen, but the air inside seemed to envelop him like heat in an oven, and to him it was heaven. He started to shiver uncontrollably, even as his clothes began thawing and dripping water onto the floor.

Kitty took him by the hand and led him to the fireplace. "Here, Skye, let me get these wet things off you."

Th-thanks." Kitty tugged and Fargo heaved, and between them they managed to relieve him of his hat and jacket, muffler, gloves, and scarf. He felt much freer after that.

"How long have you been holed up in here, Kitty?" He was pleased to note an abundance of wood, chopped and stacked neatly next to the fireplace.

"I guess this is the third or fourth day. I kind of lost count."

"You lost c-count?" How the hell can a body lose count of days? He was too cold to ask.

She hung his jacket over the mantel to dry, and spread his muffler and bandanna nearby. "Thank God I got the wood chopped before the snow started."

"You chopped the wood?" He guessed he'd sounded a little too incredulous when Kitty glared at him.

"Who the hell else was going to chop it?"

Since Fargo had no answer, he offered none. He was still too cold to talk, anyway.

The cabin consisted of two rooms. There wasn't.much furniture in this one, which appeared to be the main living quarters. What little furniture there was looked like it had been through too many winters already, but Skye Fargo wasn't one to complain. He was accustomed to sleeping under the stars in all kinds of weather. This cabin was luxurious by comparison, and it contained Kitty, thereby rendering it much more appealing than a solitary bed outside, even if the weather had been fine.

Another room with a ragged curtain tacked up and drawn back over the doorway revealed a bed. It looked as if someone was sleeping in it.

When his jaw thawed enough to move, Fargo asked, "That your friend Sally in there?"

He'd considered it a reasonable, even a simple, question. He guessed it wasn't when Kitty, as levelheaded a female as Fargo had ever known in his life, burst into tears.

"Here, Kitty, honey, don't cry. What's the matter? Is Sally sick or something?"

Kitty flung herself at him for the second time that day. This time, since he was no longer an ambulatory icicle, she didn't jump away again. Fargo hugged her hard, enjoying the feel of her supple flesh warming him up.

"She's sick, all right," Kitty sobbed. "She's dying, Skye! She was already sick. And then they beat her up something awful, and now she's dying! And it's all my fault!" She wailed the last sentence.

"What? Who beat her up? How's it your fault? What happened?"

"Clay Franklin. That's what happened. He happened to all of us."

"Sit down, honey, and tell me about it."

"Let me fetch you some food, Skye. You look half starved as well as half frozen."

Since he indeed was both, he nodded gratefully. While Kitty fetched a bowl and scooped some stew out of a pot hung on a spit over the fire in the fireplace, Fargo removed his boots and socks and his leather leggings. Thanks to his coat and his leggings, his britches were almost dry.

His feet were still as cold as ice, though, so he moved over to the fireplace and sat on a bearskin laid out in front of it. He aimed his feet at the fire, took the bowl of stew Kitty handed him, and ate hungrily. Kitty sat herself in a chair near him.

After he'd swallowed two bites of stew, he said, "So, tell me all about it, Kitty. Your letter said there was big trouble in Spanish Bend. I thought the place was too small for big trouble.

"You don't know New Mexico Territory," Kitty said grimly. "The whole place is trouble."

Fargo nodded. He'd been here before. What with Apaches and Comanches and outlaws and the hard land and harder weather, there wasn't a lot of peace to be found in the area.

"Why'd you leave San Antonio?"

"I wanted to open my own place. It was cheaper to do it out here, and they needed me." In spite of the state she was in, she managed a Kitty-like grin for him.

He smiled back. "You still a workin' girl, Kitty?"

"I am. And I had a swell place, too. Alfie Doolittle—you remember Alfie?"

"Sure do."

"Alfie said he'd help me."

Fargo grinned again. How could anybody ever forget Alfie? A wizened little man, Alfie had looked as old as the hills for as long as Fargo had known him, which was about as long as he'd known Kitty.

According to what Kitty had told Fargo a long time ago, she and Alfie weren't related by blood, but by affection. Alfie had played piano and tended bar in the first saloon Kitty'd ever entered, and they'd stuck together like fleas on a hound dog ever since.

As near as Fargo could tell, Alfie had never enjoyed Kitty's sexual favors. Rather, he acted as her surrogate father. Except that he didn't seem to mind that his surrogate daughter bedded other men for a living. Fargo wasn't judgmental by nature, and he didn't fault Alfie's tolerance.

"So you opened your own place in Spanish Bend with Alfie?"

Kitty nodded. "Alfie and me went in together in the business. I hired the girls and kept the books and Alfie played piano, tended bar, and acted as bouncer."

"Alfie acted as bouncer?" Fargo laughed. "Alfie's.as big as a minute, Kitty. What can he do to quell disturbances?"

"He's hard as granite, Skye Fargo. You know that as well as I do. And he can handle a gun, too. Near as well as I can."

All at once, Fargo realized that Alfie hadn't come out to say hello when he rode up to the cabin. He'd never seen Kitty without Alfie before, and a sick feeling attacked him. "Say, Kitty, where is Alfie?" He wasn't sure he wanted to know the answer.

She shrugged, hunched her shoulders, and started crying again. Fargo braced himself for the worst.

"I don't know where he is, Skye. I don't even know *how* he is." She buried her head in her hands and sobbed.

Fargo felt terrible. He'd always liked Alfie. "You think he might be dead?" he asked gently, afraid of sending Kitty more deeply into melancholy.

Kitty shook her head, not in denial, but to let him know she had no notion as to the state of Alfie's health. "I know they beat him up. He was laid up in bed for a long time, and I was tending to him, but I had to get out of town a week ago, and I haven't seen him since."

For some time, Fargo had been vaguely aware of a soft rattling sound, almost like the scrape of metal against metal, coming from somewhere inside the cabin. The howling wind almost rendered the scraping noise inaudible. He heard it again now. This time, it was followed by a loud groan. Then he heard the person in the other room cough twice and begin to cry feebly.

"Oh, Lord, I'd better go see if Sally needs more hot rocks in her bed. She's real bad off, Skye."

She sounded like it. Fargo rose and set his empty stew bowl on a rickety table. "Maybe there's something I can do to help."

Kitty gave him a look that told him how grateful she was for his words, and how little she believed either of them would be able to do anything for poor Sally Brown. Another miserable groan confirmed Kitty's prognosis for her friend's health.

They went to the other room. Fargo winced when Kitty pulled the blanket down to reveal the patient.

Fargo grunted involuntarily. He'd seen the results of beatings before. Hell, he'd administered enough of them and received his fair share. Until this minute, he'd not seen a woman so badly battered. He hurt, just looking at her poor swollen face.

They busted her arm, Skye, and a couple of ribs. I think what's really bad, though, is that they kicked her. I think her spleen's busted."

Fargo shook his head, unable to think of anything to say. He had some laudanum in his pack. It wouldn't save Sally's life, but it might make the leaving of it less painful. "I'm sorry, Kitty. I wish there was something I could do, but the only thing I can offer is laudanum."

"That might help ease the pain some, anyhow. Other than that, I reckon the only thing we can do for her now is to try to make her comfortable. And maybe pray."

They exchanged a glance. Fargo nodded. Sally's condition was hopeless, and he knew it as well as Kitty did. Neither one of them was much on prayer; he knew that, too.

He swore silently to himself and to Kitty and Sally Brown that he'd avenge the poor woman's death. Whoever Clay Franklin was, the bastard was going to pay for this.